P9-CCG-118

The Hope Chest of Arabella King

The Hope Chest of Arabella King

Storybook written by
Linda Zwicker

Based on the Sullivan Films Production
written by Heather Conkie
adapted from the novels of

Lucy Maud Montgomery

HarperCollins*Publishers*Ltd

THE HOPE CHEST OF ARABELLA KING
Storybook written by Linda Zwicker

Copyright © 1991 by HarperCollins Publishers Ltd,
Sullivan Films Distribution Inc., and
Ruth Macdonald and David Macdonald

Based on the Sullivan Films Production produced by Sullivan Films Inc.
in association with CBC and the Disney Channel with the participation of
Telefilm Canada adapted from Lucy Maud Montgomery's novels.

Teleplay written by Heather Conkie
Copyright © 1989 by Sullivan Films Distribution Inc.

No part of this publication may be reproduced, stored in a retrieval
system or transmitted, in any form or by any means, without the prior
permission of the Publisher, or in the case of photocopying or other
reprographic copying, a license from Canadian Reprography Collective.
For information address HarperCollins Publishers Ltd, Suite 2900,
Hazelton Lanes, 55 Avenue Road,
Toronto, Canada M5R 3L2.

Canadian Cataloguing in Publication Data
Zwicker, Linda
The hope chest of Arabella King
(Road to Avonlea; #10)
Based on the t.v. series: Road to Avonlea.
ISBN 0-00-647043-2
I. Title. II. Series.
PS8599.W53H6 1991   jC813'.54   C91-094211-0
PZ7.Z85Ho 1991

Design by Andrew Smith Graphics Inc.
91 92 93 94 95 OFF 10 9 8 7 6 5 4 3 2 1

Chapter One

"I'll bet you a hen's tooth I'm sitting on a tragedy," Sara declared cheerfully. Sara loved tragedies, especially if they involved, as her Aunt Hetty would say, "affairs of the heart."

Felicity didn't miss a stitch on the pinafore she was mending. "Gambling is a sin and hens don't have teeth. And anyway, you're only sitting on Aunt Arabella's old blue chest that's been taking up room in the corner of our kitchen forever and ever—"

"—and ever, so help me God, Amen!" added Felix, somewhat raucously.

Felicity looked up sharply. "Felix King, that's blast—blast—Anyway, you shouldn't say such things. And stop eating those gingersnaps! They're for later."

Felix popped a last bite in his mouth and proceeded to look angelic.

"That's right, you shouldn't say such things," added ten-year-old Cecily. Felicity was mending Cecily's pinafore, as a favor, and Cecily had made an all-day promise to be nice to her older sister.

Sara smiled at her cousins. "The word is *blasphemy*, Felicity. And I truly think it's too beautiful a day for anyone to get upset, especially God."

Sara gazed out the window of the large King kitchen towards the garden and the orchard beyond. The foot of the garden was bordered by a handsome lilac hedge in full bloom. Sara watched her Aunt Janet as she moved along the drooping bushes, gathering fragrant sprays of tiny, mauve blossoms.

It truly was a scrumptious day, thought Sara. Spring had waltzed into Avonlea, picked every tree and shrub for a dance partner and joyfully dressed them in perfumed blossoms of pink and white, yellow and purple. In town and in the countryside, in every house and shed, barn and loft, the sun warmed and gladdened the hearts of men, women and children.

Animals, too, felt the warmth and stirring of life. At Rose Cottage, Sara's cat Topsy stretched out on the back porch in the morning sun, purring and rumbling. He had just settled into a delicious, drowsy nap when Hetty King marched out onto the porch to beat the parlor rugs. Hetty saw this day as the ideal opportunity to engage in some brisk spring housecleaning.

She was about to shoo Topsy away, as she always did, when she suddenly paused. Bending down, Hetty scratched his warm, silky ears. He closed his eyes in ecstasy and rolled over. Hetty inwardly chided herself for wasting time petting a cat when she should be spring cleaning, but nonetheless, she kept on until Topsy's purring reached alarming proportions.

On the front porch of Rose Cottage, Sara's Aunt Olivia sat in the yellow rocking chair, re-reading a letter. She didn't really have to read it, because she knew it all by heart. The letter read:

> Dear Miss King,
>
> I received your poem "Season's End." I am happy to tell you that it will appear in the Avonlea *Chronicle* on Saturday, May 28th. I enclose a cheque for $1.00. Thank you for thinking of submitting your writing to our paper.
>
> Yours faithfully,
> Quentin Tyler,
> Editor and Publisher

"Thank you for thinking of submitting your writing to our paper!" For some reason, that line pleased Aunt Olivia tremendously. It seemed to suggest that she had so many places she could submit her work—vast oceans of possibilities, from the Charlottetown *Journal* to the Halifax *Echo* to the Toronto *Women's Guide* and that out of all of these, she had chosen their very own Avonlea *Chronicle* to publish her first poem.

Her first poem! And today she would see it in print. As soon as Sara came back from visiting her King cousins, they would set off to town to get a copy of the *Chronicle*. Or maybe two copies, one for Olivia's scrapbook and one for just "having around."

Olivia smiled to herself as she remembered how excited Sara had been when Olivia showed her the letter from Quentin Tyler.

"See, I told you!" cried Sara. "I told you if you submitted it, they'd publish it."

"Oh, Sara, you were right," admitted Olivia, hugging her niece close. "And I'll tell you what we're going to do. We're going to cash that cheque and let you pick out whatever you want from Lawson's store."

Sara's eyes shone. "Truly?"

"Truly," confirmed Olivia. "On Saturday, when we go to pick up the paper."

Sara glowed. "Thank you, Aunt Olivia. Now tell me, what does Aunt Hetty think of your poem?"

Aunt Olivia's clear face clouded for just a moment. "I want it to be a surprise for Hetty," Olivia said. She lowered her voice a little. "Sometimes I think Aunt Hetty needs more surprises in her life, don't you?"

Sara hesitated.

"So let's keep it our secret, all right, Sara?"

They smiled a little wickedly at each other.

"It's a promise," confirmed Sara. "I love secrets."

Felicity's pretty mouth had a determined set. "No, Sara, it's absolutely better to know something than not to know." She folded Cecily's pinafore carefully and added it to her "mending-done" pile on the kitchen table. Felicity, thirteen years old, was the eldest of the King children, and she took her household responsibilities very seriously.

"Felicity's right," echoed Cecily, remembering her all-day promise. "What do you think, Mother?"

Janet was just placing the last of the lilacs in a lovely white milk pitcher. "I don't know, dear," she replied, dreamily admiring the handsome flowers.

"Mother," pressed Felicity, "what *do* you think about secrets?"

Janet snapped back to reality and reached for

the kettle. "What I think is that I need a cup of tea."

"I still think secrets are best," mused Sara, enjoying the scent of the lilacs as their rich fragrance rolled through the kitchen and drifted out the open door.

"Then why do you want to know everything about Aunt Arabella's blue chest?" challenged Felix, as he plunked down beside Sara.

"Yes, why?" queried Cecily, looking at Sara earnestly.

"Well," replied Sara, "even when a person thinks they know everything, there's still always something hidden. A secret goes on forever and ever."

Cecily was puzzled. "Is that true, Mother?"

Janet stood at the kitchen counter, nibbling one of Felicity's spicy gingersnaps, "testing its flavor," as she told Felicity. Janet told herself she shouldn't eat quite so many gingersnaps. This morning she had put on one of her lighter dresses from last year, and the waistband was snug, very snug.

"Aunt Janet," pressed Sara, "why has this chest never been opened?"

"Because of death and horrible destruction," intoned Felix dramatically. Cecily giggled.

"It's not funny," warned their mother. "It's tragic."

"I love—"

"We know, Sara," interrupted Felicity, rolling her eyes skyward, "you *love* tragedies."

"Tragedies stand among the finest literary works of mankind," stated Sara firmly. Janet reached for yet another gingersnap, possibly, thought Sara, to fortify herself to tell the story of Arabella.

Chapter Two

"This all happened fifty years ago, before my time," Janet assured them. "Aunt Arabella was the youngest sister of Grandfather King."

"Was she beautiful?" asked Felicity, to whom such things were quite important.

"Not really, but people said there was a kind of lightness and grace about her. She was one of those people who is blessed with a kind of natural charm. And apparently she was a fine elocutionist. Her outstanding performance piece was 'The Lady of the Lake.'"

"I know that poem!" cried Sara. "It's in the *Sixth Royal Reader*." She cleared her throat and paused theatrically.

"The stag at eve had drunk his fill,
where danced the moon on Monan's rill,
And deep his midnight lair had made,
In lone Glenartney's hazel shade."

Felix's eyes widened. "You know the very same poem as Aunt Arabella!"

"When you get to sixth grade, you'll have to learn it too, Felix," Felicity reminded him crisply. "Mother, please continue."

"Aunt Arabella was engaged to be married, to a very fine young man called Will."

"Sweet William," murmured Sara, "just like the flower."

"At any rate, the most dreadful, dreadful thing happened. The very morning of their wedding, a lovely day much like this, Will was found dead. He had been shot through the heart."

The children gasped. Felicity's voice quavered. "You never told us he'd been shot."

"Until now I felt you were too young to know," Janet acknowledged. "But that's the very truth of it."

"Murdered stone, cold dead," nodded Felix. "I'm not surprised."

"Oh, no, Felix," said his mother. "It wasn't murder. It was suicide, I'm afraid. A very sad business."

"Poor Arabella," whispered Sara.

Janet poured her tea and, after only a moment's hesitation, added two lumps of sugar.

"When Arabella heard the news she said nothing. Poor soul, she was probably in shock. Be that as it may, she took her wedding dress, her veil and I don't know what else, and locked them away in this trunk. Then she ran off to Halifax on the train, taking the key with her."

"Did she ever come back to Avonlea?" asked Sara.

"Not so far. But she's still alive, although she's well on in her eighties. I believe her health is failing."

"Oh, I'd love to meet her," confessed Sara.

"She won't see anyone, Sara," noted Felicity.

"That's true," confirmed Janet. "It's her wish and must be respected. We exchange cards at Christmas, but it's never more than the usual greetings. Aunt Arabella only wrote once, when she got to Halifax all those years ago. She said we must promise never, ever to open the blue chest."

Sara rapped on the chest. "Maybe it's cursed." Felix's eyes twinkled in enthusiastic agreement.

"Oh, I don't think it's cursed. I think it's just full of memories. Long-ago memories."

Sara felt the wood of the old trunk, warm to her hand. A tragic love story, a shooting, and a mystery, all wrapped up together! Arabella and Will— aching, star-crossed lovers. Sara smiled. It was like a poem. A poem! She jumped up. The morning had flown by, and Aunt Olivia would be waiting impatiently for her.

"Ouch!" yelped Felicity, as Sara accidentally jumped on her toe. "Where are you going, Sara?"

"On an adventure!" shouted Sara, as she ran out into the spring sunshine. "And I'm late!"

Sarah sped along the lane, streaking past the old King orchard, where fragrant white apple blossoms bowed their greetings as she rushed by. Suddenly, she stopped dead in her tracks. Leaping leapfrogs, she thought, I know Aunt Olivia is waiting for me, but honestly and truly, how many days like this ever come along in the world?

It seemed almost rude to twelve-year-old Sara to rush by the budding trees and clusters of pink and white mayflowers that starred the newly green fields of Avonlea. She breathed deeply of the sweet spring air and proceeded to walk, arms swinging, down the hill, hopping across the shiny stones that bridged the brook and skipping past Jasper Dale's house, Golden Milestone.

Well, actually, Sara didn't quite skip past Jasper Dale's house, because she paused a moment to speak to him as he planted tulip bulbs in his large flower garden. Everyone in town called Jasper Dale "the Awkward Man," when they called him anything at all, that is. Jasper participated little in the social life of the community and kept pretty much to himself, so his name didn't come up often in conversation or gossip down at Lawson's store.

"Good morning, Mr. Dale," Sara called cheerfully.

Jasper reddened, ducked and stammered all in one jerky motion. "Oh, M-Miss—Miss Stanley, h-h-hello." He glanced up quickly at Sara and then turned again to his tulip bulbs, staring at them with fierce intensity.

Sara smiled. "Isn't this a dream of a day?"

Jasper bobbed and re-settled the wire-rimmed glasses that had slipped down his long, plain nose. Jasper Dale was a plain man, no doubt about it. Although he was tall and slim, he was the kind of a person who seemed to melt into the background. Which is just the way Jasper liked it, because he was shy. Painfully shy. Excruciatingly shy. Mrs. Griggs, who came in to clean Golden Milestone once a week, declared that the Awkward Man was "as shy as a calf at noon." No one was quite sure what that meant, but it sounded definite.

Jasper, who was about forty, lived alone, and had since his mother passed away some ten years before, leaving him to run the farm. He was an adequate farmer, but his real passions were gardening, repairing things and photography. Sara knew that Jasper Dale had outfitted his barn as a combination darkroom, library and photography studio. She even had the good fortune to see it for herself. "As neat as a pin," Mrs. Griggs confirmed, "A place for everything and everything in its place."

Sara leaned on the fence, watching Jasper as he dug up the red, rich earth, his stooping back bent to the task. The sun warmed her face. A jolly robin landed on the fence beside her, chirped and flew off to watch events from a nearby tree.

"I'm just on my way to pick up Aunt Olivia and Aunt Hetty and we're going into town, and do you know what, Mr. Dale?" Sara waited. "Do you know what?"

Jasper gulped and shook his head. "Wh-wh-wh—?" He sputtered to a halt.

Sara decided to put him out of his misery. "We're going to pick up a copy of the Avonlea *Chronicle* because there's an amazing surprise in it. An amazing surprise that has to do with Aunt Olivia."

"Tha-that's good. Your Aunt—Aunt Olivia is a very—"

He looked up at Sara and smiled, slightly. Jasper Dale's smile was warm and sincere. It lit up his intelligent, deep-blue eyes and softened his angular features. It was a smile you could trust, a smile you could believe in. It was a smile that the mention of Aunt Olivia had inspired. And as suddenly as a summer storm, it hit Sara—Jasper Dale liked Aunt Olivia!

Well, of course, thought Sara, why shouldn't he? After all, Aunt Olivia wasn't too, too old—twenty-nine to be exact. And besides, Aunt Olivia had a warm, true heart and a bubbling, rather shy sense of humor. Not to mention that she was, as Sara put it, "as pretty as a pansy." In fact, it was a bit of a mystery to Sara why Aunt Olivia wasn't already married, but she had once overheard Aunt Hetty say that there simply wasn't a "gentleman of quality" in Avonlea that could measure up to the King standards. So Aunt Olivia kept busy with baking and bazaars and the Literary Society and kindliness to neighbors and keeping house for Aunt Hetty and Sara at Rose Cottage.

But Sara thought that the best thing of all about Aunt Olivia was that under her fair breast beat the heart of a poet. That made her a kindred spirit. And Sara suspected that the Awkward Man had a bit of a poetic streak, too. Once she had seen him reading a book of Byron's poems at the Literary Society, when he was supposed to be listening to a rather tedious talk by Reverend Leonard. Oh yes, Aunt Olivia and Jasper Dale would make a perfect couple, no doubt about it. And Aunt Olivia, or rather Mrs. Jasper Dale, would move into Golden Milestone, and the house would be full of light and poetry and music, and they would ask, no, *insist*, that Sara come to live with them and—

"Arrgh," grunted Jasper Dale, wiping some dirt from his face. He turned to Sara, embarrassed. Being a bit dreamy, he'd forgotten she was there.

Sara smiled. "Mr. Dale, I must be running along. Aunt Olivia will be waiting. Perhaps you'll be in town later?"

The Awkward Man regarded the tulip bulbs. "I—I—who—who knows?" he finally managed to stammer.

"Oh, I know," laughed Sara, as she skipped away. "A very good day to you, Mr. Dale."

Chapter Three

Hetty and Olivia had donned their summer straw hats and were anxiously watching for Sara from the front porch. They marched briskly to meet her as she ran up the lane.

"Really, Sara," chided her Aunt Hetty, "it is discourteous to be late when, with just a little thought, you could be on time. Your Aunt Olivia was getting very upset."

Olivia smiled forgivingly at Sara. "It's all right, Hetty. After all, it is Saturday, and a few minutes here or there don't really matter."

Hetty sailed on. "It's not just a matter of punctuality, it's a matter of keeping one's word. A promise made should be a promise kept."

Sara had to walk quickly to keep up with her two aunts as they strode along the road.

"I'm sorry, Aunt Hetty, truly I am, but I fell into a conversation. A wonderful conversation."

"Really," chirped Olivia. "Who with?"

"With whom" corrected Hetty, "with *whom*?"

"With Jasper Dale!" trumpeted Sara.

Hetty adjusted the brim of her hat. "Well, I'm rather surprised to hear that, Sara, since Mr. Dale seems quite incapable of having a conversation, wonderful or otherwise. The man's a social incompetent."

"Oh no, Hetty," countered Olivia. "He's just very, very shy."

"He's just very, very strange," Hetty said decidedly.

"What do you mean?" asked Sara.

"I shouldn't repeat rumors..."

"Oh, please, please Aunt Hetty. I won't tell anyone, ever, oh, please?"

"Well," confided Hetty, "Mrs. Griggs tells an odd tale about the Awkward Man, a very odd tale indeed."

"Mrs. Griggs is a gossip and a troublemaker," warned Olivia.

"Well, of course she is, Olivia. I'm only telling Sara what she said, not supporting her account. At any rate, one day when she was cleaning the Awkward Man's house, she came upon a room under the west gable. Now usually this room was locked, but Mrs. Griggs, being Mrs. Griggs, always tried the door, and this particular time she found it open."

Sara's eyes widened. "And?"

"Well, I can tell you, she found some very interesting things there. Very interesting, indeed."

Sara could scarcely contain herself. "What did she find, Aunt Hetty, what?!"

"It's only idle talk, Sara, but it seems the room was furnished in a peculiar way. A way not in keeping with a bachelor's house, one might say."

"I don't understand," wailed Sara.

"There's nothing to understand," insisted Olivia. "Everyone is entitled to their privacy, and especially a person as private as Jasper Dale. Really, Hetty, I'm surprised at you, spreading such talk."

"Oh, I see Mr. Dale has a champion," teased Hetty. "My, my."

"Jasper Dale is a lovely man, isn't he, Aunt Olivia?" asked Sara.

Olivia blushed, or maybe it was just the noon sun beating down on her fair face.

"I think 'lovely' is a rather extreme word to describe Jasper Dale, Sara," cautioned Hetty. "But then you're young and rather impressionable."

With that, Hetty reached into the deep pocket of her long skirt, pulled out her shopping list, checked it and would talk no more of the Awkward Man and strangely furnished rooms.

Lawson's general store was one of Sara's favorite places, especially on a busy Saturday. All kinds of folks gathered there to chat and exchange news of the town. If you were lucky, you heard things that were not, as Aunt Hetty said, "suitable for young ears."

In addition to foodstuffs and fabrics and candles and the like, Lawson's store contained an amazing selection of delicious, intriguing candies. Butterscotch twists and lemon drops and salt-water taffy, golden and tempting, were housed in large glass containers lining the back counter. In the third jar from the left was Sara's favorite, "Cupid's Whispers." "Cupids," as the girls called them, were small, heart-shaped, violet candies, flavored with licorice and dusted with sugar.

But right now, Sara was more interested in something else on the counter, the Avonlea *Chronicle.* As soon as she entered the store, she made a beeline for it. But before she could reach it,

Mrs. Lawson snatched the newspaper and held it high, waving it like a signal flag.

"Oh, Olivia," she gushed, "I must say I enjoyed your poem in the newspaper so very much."

Olivia smiled shyly and bit her lip. "It's in? My poem is actually in the newspaper?"

Mrs. Lawson surrendered the newspaper to Olivia, who immediately spread it out on the counter. She and Sara quickly scanned the pages.

"Poem?" sniffed Hetty, "What poem?"

"Oh, dear yes, Hetty," trilled Mrs. Lawson. "I read it out loud to Edward this morning, and he said that he felt right proud to be acquainted with the person who wrote it."

"There it is!" whooped Sara. "'Season's End,'" by Olivia J. King! Oh, Aunt Olivia, I'm so proud of you."

"You never told me about this, Olivia," said Hetty sharply. "You never breathed a word."

Olivia's eyes shone. "Well, there it is. My name in print. I can't believe it."

Aunt Hetty snorted. "'Season's End'? That's a rather common sentiment, I should think. Really, Olivia."

Mrs. Lawson drew herself erect and cleared her throat. "I quite liked the part where Olivia wrote—" At this point Mrs. Lawson paused and lifted one hand, as though shielding her eyes from the sun.

"'As winter's bitter snows run laughing to the sea, so spring...'" Mrs. Lawson scrunched up her face, groping for the words, "'so spring...'"

"'So spring in all her glory, a dazzling maid must be!'" finished Sara, with a flourish.

"Yes, quite," confirmed Mrs. Lawson, rather crisply. "At any rate, Olivia, your poem was a welcome change from the usual reports of the comings and goings of Avonlea. If you ask me, the newspaper's gone downhill since old Mr. Tyler died, don't you agree, Hetty?"

Hetty was inspecting a barrel of apples and scarcely seemed to hear.

"Well, I never considered the *Chronicle* to be of particular merit at any time, Elvira."

"Well, it never was as good as the Charlottetown *Evening News*, that's certain, but I think it's deteriorated even more since Mr. Tyler's son took over. Olivia, you should think about doing more writing for it. It could use some new blood."

"I could use a pound of imported English breakfast tea, Elvira, if you don't mind," directed Hetty, a bit chuffily.

Olivia smiled at Sara and opened her tiny velvet purse. She held out a one-dollar bill—her "poem money."

"Now, Sara, what can I buy you with my ill-gotten gains?"

Sara grinned. "Oh, Cupids, please!"

"Elvira, half a pound of Cupids, if you please," commanded Aunt Olivia. "They're quite the rage, aren't they?"

"That old witch Peg Bowen says that if you eat three before bed, you'll dream of your true love," confided Sara.

Hetty raised an eyebrow. "Why three?"

"One for yourself, one for your intended and the third is Cupid's arrow between the two. Isn't that romantic?" sighed Sara.

"It's lovely," confirmed Olivia.

"Well," remarked Hetty, "with two dreamers in the family, it's a good thing that someone has a practical head on her shoulders. I don't know what you two would do without me. As Grandfather King used to say, 'Some will dance, while others hoe.'"

"Hoe?" repeated Sara.

"Indeed," said Hetty. "Hoe, hoe, hoe."

Maybe it was the bubbling day, maybe it was Aunt Olivia's poem, maybe it was just life doing a handstand, but Aunt Hetty seriously repeating "hoe" struck Sara as terribly funny, and she burst into laughter. She simply couldn't help herself. Her merry peals caught up Olivia and Mrs. Lawson, and even Hetty smiled a bit stiffly, as she paid for the groceries.

Chapter Four

Quentin Tyler was bent over his printer's desk, closely examining a double page of type, hunting for errors. As he spoke, he barely glanced up through his green eyeshade.

"Yes, ladies, what can I do for you today?"

Sara wondered how the world would look, viewed through a green eyeshade. Probably like being under a great, green, wandering ocean.

Olivia gulped. "Mr. Tyler, I'm Olivia King." She waited, expecting a response. There wasn't one. "I wrote 'Season's End.'"

Mr. Tyler leaned back. "Ah, yes, the poet."

Olivia looked flustered. "I was, that is, we were wondering—"

Hetty took charge. "Mr. Tyler, my sister wishes to purchase two copies of today's *Chronicle*, if you please."

"Three copies, Aunt Hetty," whispered Sara. "One to mail to father." Sara's father was away, trying to clear his name of false charges brought against him in connection with his business, Stanley Imports. That was why Sara was living, for the time being, on the Island with her late mother's relatives.

"Certainly," said Mr. Tyler, sliding off his high stool and approaching the front counter.

Quentin Tyler was a fairly young man, with even features, curly dark hair and unsmiling gray eyes. He handed Olivia three copies. "Fifteen cents, please."

"Mr. Tyler, I want to thank you for publishing my work," said Olivia, passing him the coins.

"Don't thank me, Miss King. I'm not some high-brow Toronto publisher attempting to produce works of lasting literary importance. I'm just the publisher of the Avonlea *Chronicle*. Printing your poem was a business decision, nothing more."

An uncomfortable silence fell. Hetty picked it up.

"I knew your father, Mr. Tyler. I was sorry to hear he passed away."

"My father ended his days a bitter man who left me unpleasant memories and a debt-ridden news-paper. Now, if you'll excuse me, I must get back to work. Good day, ladies."

He turned his back to them, leaving his visitors no option but to leave as quickly as they could.

"Really," growled Hetty when they were back out on the street. "What an ungracious young man."

"I don't know, Aunt Hetty," said Sara. "I thought his eyes were sad—deep down, I mean."

"Well, child, you do look for the best in people, I'll say that for you."

Sara spotted someone shambling along the street towards them, someone she was delighted to see.

"Aunt Olivia," Sara whispered, "look who's coming."

When Jasper Dale looked up and saw Olivia King, with Sara and Hetty, outside the newspaper office, his immediate instinct was to wheel around and walk in the other direction, or cross the street, or—

"Hello, Mr. Dale!" Sara waved enthusiastically.

Olivia lowered her voice. "Sara, please, I don't think Mr. Dale—"

"Here we are!" hallooed Sara. The Awkward Man blushed as he moved towards them.

Janet King stood transfixed, on the post office steps, holding a letter in front of her. She gasped dramatically.

"Well, did ever any mortal—"

"What is it, Ma?" pressed Felix. "You look as red as a Cavendish lobster."

Janet handed the lawyer's letter to her husband Alec. "Your Aunt Arabella is dead."

"My goodness," exclaimed Alec King. "I had forgotten she was alive."

"Father, how could you say such a thing!" scolded Felicity.

"Is it sad?" asked Cecily.

"Look," said Alec, holding up a large brass key, which glinted in the bright sunshine.

"Jumping Jehoshaphat!" yelled Felix. "It's the key to Aunt Arabella's blue chest! Hurray!"

Janet King shot her son a look that would have frozen a pirate's blood.

"Felix, your Aunt Arabella was a close relative. What do you mean by such behavior?"

"I wasn't hurraying because she's dead, Ma. I hurrayed because we finally get to open that blue chest. Let's go home and open it right now!"

"Oh, yes, can we please, Mother?" echoed Cecily, in a small voice.

"Wait till Sara hears this," crowed Felicity. "Now *this* is a real adventure."

Janet sat down on the post office bench and fanned herself with the letter. Felicity, Felix and Cecily crowded around her, chattering excitedly.

"Hush, hush," ordered Janet. "Now, let me think, let me think."

"We don't have all day, dear," observed Alec.

"I think," said Janet, "since every family member is to be given a remembrance from Aunt Arabella's chest, that we should have a dinner, a special family dinner "

"I'll make jam roly-poly," offered Felicity.

"That would be nice, dear," said her mother, "and we'll invite Aunt Hetty and Aunt Olivia and Sara, and then after dinner, we'll all gather and open the chest. How does that sound?"

Cecily's eyes shone. "I can hardly wait until tonight!"

"Oh, no dear," said Janet. "The day after tomorrow is the earliest we can organize a big dinner like that."

"But the day after tomorrow is ages away!" bawled Felix.

"Well," said Janet crisply, "Aunt Arabella's chest has been locked up for fifty years. I doubt if two more nights will make a difference."

"Let's go and find Sara," commanded Felicity. "I can hardly wait to see the look on her face!" With that, the three children bounded down the street, eager to find their cousin and share the exciting news.

"We'll be at Lawson's store," their mother called after them, but her voice was lost in the warm breeze.

"See, I told you, Aunt Olivia," trumpeted Sara, "I told you Jasper Dale would like your poem."

"Oh, Sara," said Olivia, as they strolled down the street towards home. "What could the poor man say, when you asked him directly like that?"

"Indeed," added Hetty, "it's in poor taste to ask such a question outright, Sara."

"He did like it, Aunt Hetty," insisted Sara, "I could tell."

"Well, I hope so," replied Olivia, softly.

"But he likes *you*, Aunt Olivia," declared Sara, "not just your poem."

"Really, where do you get such ideas?" Aunt Olivia shook her head, but looked rather pleased all the same.

Sara said nothing, but remembered Jasper Dale's smile in the garden.

Then, suddenly, her world went dark! The street disappeared! Avonlea disappeared! From behind, a pair of small, grubby hands had clamped down on her eyes.

"Felix King!" Sara shrieked, grabbing Felix's hands as she spun round. "What do you think you're doing!!"

Felix, Felicity and Cecily held their arms straight out from their bodies, squeezed their eyes shut, swayed, and chanted together, "The chest. The chest will be opened. Death and treasure and Aunt Arabella's ghost will arise. All will be revealed."

Sara's eyes widened. "What are you talking about?"

With that, the children broke into laughter and proceeded to tell Sara and Hetty and Olivia all about the letter and the key and, of course, the splendid dinner that would make it, as Sara decreed, "a Grand Occasion."

"What do you think is in the chest, Sara?" asked Cecily, looking quite grave.

"Aunt Arabella herself," said Sara earnestly.

Everyone gasped. Felix found his voice first. "Wh-what do you mean?"

"I mean," explained Sara, "her spirit. Her spirit is woven into everything in the chest. All her hopes and dreams and fears she laid in that chest and locked away, just as surely as she laid down her china and embroidery and whatever else we'll find in there."

Chapter Five

Aunt Hetty pulled back the curtains of Sara's cosy bedroom. Sunlight splashed in, filling every corner.

"Sara, for goodness sake, wake up!" she called, shaking Sara's shoulder. "Breakfast is on the table and you'll be late for school, my girl, if you don't shake a leg."

"Oh, Aunt Hetty," confided Sara, "I was having the most wonderful, strange dream."

"Well, dreams are dreams, child, but hard work is what makes dreams come true."

"Well," noted Sara, rubbing her eyes, "you have to have dreams first." Peg Bowen was right. Three Cupids before bed was just the ticket!

Hetty paused and looked at Sara. "You look—" She stopped herself.

Sara hopped out of bed. "What, Aunt Hetty?"

Hetty's voice softened. "Nothing, child. It's just that you look quite like your mother at times."

"Do I? Truly? Because Mama was lovely, wasn't she?"

"Well, all the King sisters have their strong points, but Ruth had several combined."

"Aunt Olivia told me Mama used to tell stories, wonderful yarns."

"Oh, yes," confirmed Hetty. "Your mother was a dreamer, like you. She had an enchanting voice, and in the evening we would gather in the parlor round the fire, and how she would make us laugh, oh my, and cry, too..."

A distant, sad look settled on Hetty's sharp features. It was a look that Sara saw rarely, but it said, in a way words couldn't, how dearly Hetty had loved Sara's mother.

"Aunt Hetty, sometimes you look like Mother, too," Sara murmured.

Aunt Hetty snapped back to the realities of the moment and consulted the watch pinned to the bodice of her crisp, white, cotton blouse.

"I want you downstairs in five minutes, child. And don't forget to iron your red pinafore when you get home from school. We must be suitably dressed for dinner and the grand opening of Aunt Arabella's blue chest this evening."

"Oh, yes!" cried Sara, as she started to brush her hair. It was Monday, and Aunt Janet's dinner was tonight."The Grand Occasion! I wonder what we'll find. Maybe we'll solve the mystery of Aunt Arabella and Will, star-crossed lovers that they were."

Once Sara had washed and dressed, she rushed down to the kitchen. A large bowl of steaming oatmeal porridge, laced with Jamaican molasses, looked up at her. She sighed a mighty sigh.

"Oh, Aunt Hetty, must I eat this? I thought since it was summer, I could just have toast for breakfast."

"It's spring, Sara, and we can't risk you getting sick. Oatmeal fortifies one against illness," proclaimed Hetty, as she gathered up her books for school. As the Avonlea schoolmistress, it would not do for Hetty to be late.

Olivia placed another bowl of oatmeal on the table. "I'll keep you company, Sara," she said, sitting down and spreading the Avonlea *Chronicle* out on the checkered cloth.

Hetty's eyebrows shot up. "Olivia, *please* don't read at the table!"

Olivia laughed. "It's only breakfast, Hetty. Don't worry, none of the neighbors will see."

"I suppose you're reading your poem for the umpteenth time. I think we're all quite aware that you're now a published author, Olivia. There's no need to put on airs."

A look of real anger crossed Olivia's face. "I'm not, Hetty! That was an uncalled-for remark."

Hetty sniffed. "Well, I'm only concerned for your welfare, Olivia. Really, why would you waste your time writing poetic frippery? I tell you, you're getting to be more and more of a dreamer. You should have more get-up-and-go, more of the King practicality."

"Speaking of dreaming, Aunt Olivia," said Sara, who had so far managed to avoid eating any of her oatmeal. "Last night I dreamt that you married Jasper Dale. I was a bridesmaid, and—"

"Too many Cupids," teased Aunt Olivia.

"I would consider marrying Jasper Dale to be a nightmare, not a dream," observed Hetty. "Well, I must be off to school. I have the spelling quiz to prepare. I'll see you both later." With that, Aunt Hetty said goodbye and closed the door firmly behind her. A small, lovely silence settled on the warm kitchen.

Sara had the feeling that Aunt Olivia wanted to know about her dream, so she volunteered every little detail. Actually, she rather embroidered the story, building it into quite an event. By the time Sara had finished, you could almost hear the merry church bells pealing as the marriage was celebrated throughout the town!

Olivia rose from the table and started to clear away the breakfast dishes, a small smile still playing around her pretty lips. Sara looked down at the newspaper, which was open to the "Positions Available" section.

"Aunt Olivia, listen to this!" Sara commanded. She read aloud, "Newspaper position available at the Avonlea *Chronicle*. Please apply in person to Quentin Tyler, Publisher."

"My goodness," said Olivia. "I didn't think Mr. Tyler could afford to hire anyone."

"Aunt Olivia," declared Sara, "you must apply for the job."

Olivia laughed out loud. "Me?"

Sara nodded vigorously. "Yes, you."

Aunt Olivia shook her head as she scrubbed out the porridge pot. "One minute you have me married to Jasper Dale, the next I'm a reporter. Really, Sara, you *are* a dreamer."

"No, I'm not! You know how to write, and you could really show Aunt Hetty that you've got some of that famous King 'get-up-and-go.'"

"I don't know, Sara. It's a big decision."

Sara reached for a tea towel and started to dry the old, blue-enameled porridge pot.

"I know. But 'determination is the key to success.' That's what Grandfather King used to say."

"I never heard him say that," replied Olivia.

"Well, if he didn't, he should have," chirped Sara.

Chapter Six

Olivia King brushed the flour from the front of her red gingham apron and sat down at the kitchen table. This morning, in addition to baking bread, Olivia had created a tray of fragrant cinnamon buns, which she hoped would be a delicious addition to Janet's dinner later on. Topsy threaded, warm and furry, through Olivia's ankles. If I didn't know what day of the week it was, Olivia thought, I would just have to look at the bread pans, because Monday is always baking day.

Now it wasn't that Olivia disliked making bread, it was just that today, for some reason, Olivia felt the weight of routine, of the "King traditions." There was a whole world out there, she thought, where people were doing exciting things, like exploring the tombs of Egyptian pharaohs, or riding horses through dangerous mountain passes, or sailing in warm, azure oceans or falling in love. Falling in love—goodness, what had brought that thought to mind?

Olivia had been in love once, with Edwin Clarke. But looking back on it, maybe she hadn't *really* been in love. If she had, then why had she let Hetty interfere in the matter? Hetty, meaning well, had said that Edwin Clarke was a young man with "few prospects," and that she worried deeply about Olivia's relationship with him. So Olivia broke off with Edwin. Promptly thereafter he went off to Parkville, married Tilly, a plump, Simpson girl, and they'd settled down on a farm, where they were now raising three plump children.

"So maybe it wasn't love," Olivia confessed to her bread pans.

And then there was this business with Jasper Dale. Olivia had known Jasper her whole life and had never really thought about him, one way or the other. He was like a piece of comfortable furniture, nice enough to have about, but not necessary to one's existence. All the same, lately Olivia had found Jasper more and more in her thoughts. There was a kind of goodness and honesty about Jasper. It wasn't so much what he said, for the man certainly wasn't one for speechifying, but it was the way Jasper lived his life. That's where the honesty was. He didn't engage in petty gossip or sharp business schemes, but quietly did simple, good things for people.

Then there was his artistic side, his photography. Most folks took the usual snapshots of the ocean and the shore and the countryside, but

Jasper would take a photo of, say, a barn door, in a way that would make it look like something noble and beautiful and interesting. Whenever Jasper put his photographs up as part of the decorations for the Avonlea Harvest Festival, or contributed them for sale at the church bazaar, Olivia always looked at them attentively. They interested her. Last year she had bought one, although she never told Jasper. The photograph was of the back of a horse's head, and it was taken from a most interesting angle.

Really, thought Olivia, what am I doing sitting here on a Monday morning thinking about photographs and Jasper Dale? Maybe Hetty is right, maybe I am just a dreamer.

Olivia stood up smartly, removed her apron, hung it on the back of the door and proceeded to clear the kitchen table. She folded up the newspaper and then stopped short. Sara's words seemed to echo in the kitchen, "Newspaper position available at the Avonlea *Chronicle*. Please apply in person." Olivia paused.

"Well, why not, Topsy?" Topsy yawned. "After all, I've never had a proper job, and maybe it's time I risked doing something. Maybe it's time I took my life into my own hands, or at least tried to."

So as Sara and Felicity and the other children sweated their way through Aunt Hetty's corker of a spelling quiz Olivia changed her clothes, put on her best hat, bid Topsy goodbye and marched into town.

Quentin Tyler was busy at the printing press, and the slap and roar of the inky machine made conversation difficult. Olivia stood opposite him, trying to maintain her composure while shouting. He scarcely looked up at her as he fed paper through the press.

"I know I have very little experience, Mr. Tyler," shouted Olivia, "but I have lots of ideas."

"Everyone's full of ideas, Miss King. That's the easy part. What I need is someone to write the social notices and make them so interesting that people will actually pay money to read them."

Olivia was surprised at how determined she felt. "Mr. Tyler, I'm sure I can do that. And there are lots of other events I could write about." What on earth was she saying? If Mr. Tyler asked her in the next ten seconds what those events might be, she wouldn't be able to name even one!

"Miss King, during my father's time as publisher, people were content with the *Chronicle*, but nowadays they just want to read the big Charlottetown papers. Face it, Miss King, nothing exciting ever happens in Avonlea." With that, Mr. Tyler pulled a sample handbill from the press, brought the machine to a clanking halt and walked over to his desk. Olivia followed him.

"Mr. Tyler, surely you don't believe that nothing ever happens in Avonlea?"

Quentin Tyler looked up at Olivia, his mouth set.

"The only excitement I have is with my bank manager, who is very unhappy about my overdraft. Miss King, I've inherited a—a dead horse." His gaze returned to the handbill.

A dead horse? thought Olivia. How about a live horse, a very live horse indeed!

"Mr. Tyler, maybe if you had photographs, that would help. Now, the one thing the Charlottetown papers have is photographs. Don't you think that would make the local news much more exciting?"

"Miss King," said Mr. Tyler wearily, "I do not have photographs because I cannot afford a photographer."

"Well, if the paper were more interesting then more people would buy it, and then you *could* afford a photographer," persisted Olivia.

Mr. Tyler smiled slightly. "As simple as that, is it?"

"In fact, I'm sure I could find someone to donate their time. Avonlea is simply *full* of people with many talents. People who just never get a chance to use them."

"Is that right," commented Mr. Tyler, walking past Olivia to a nearby filing cabinet.

"Yes, that is right," said Olivia, quite boldly, to Mr. Tyler's back. He turned round and faced her.

"Well, if you think you can do it, then do it."

Olivia's heart raced. "You mean I have the job?"

"No," said Mr. Tyler. "But you find your photographer and your exciting local news and then I'll decide whether or not to take you on. How does that sound?"

Olivia's face broke into a smile. "Oh, thank you, Mr. Tyler."

"And while you're at it," he added, "don't forget the vitals."

"The vitals?"

"The births and deaths, Miss King. The only news you can rely on in this district."

"Mr. Tyler," vowed Olivia, drawing herself up to her full height, "I am going to prove you wrong."

Mr. Tyler turned back to the printing press. "Well, we'll see, Miss King, we'll see."

Chapter Seven

Sara heaved the heavy iron from the stove and applied it, with a thump, to her red pinafore.

"Oh, child," cried Hetty, "that really is too heavy for you. Here, let me do it."

"Thank you, Aunt Hetty," said Sara, looking out

the window towards the lane. "I wonder where Aunt Olivia is? We don't want to be late for dinner."

"Ever since Olivia got that poem published she's been quite unlike herself," Hetty complained. "Sara, leave those cinnamon buns alone!"

Sara licked a little bit of the delicious brown sugar mixture from her fingers.

"Is Aunt Olivia acting the way Mother used to?"

"What do you mean?"

"You know," mused Sara, "dreamy. Like she might fall in love and run off with someone."

"Sara, I think it's much healthier for young minds not to dwell in the past. Now, here's your pinafore. Run up to your room and change. I'm going on ahead to give Janet a hand with dinner, so you come along later with your Aunt Olivia. I'm sure she'll be home soon."

Sara loved her red pinafore. Her father had sent it from Paris at Christmas, along with an exquisite pair of tan kid boots. Boots that could only be made in Paris, Sara told the girls at school, so fine was their workmanship.

Sara fully acknowledged that Felicity was the beauty of their little group, no doubt about it. But one thing Sara had, in addition to her vivid imagination and story-telling talents, were very nice feet. Sara wiggled her elegant toes. What a shame that her best physical feature had to be covered up most of the time!

Up in her bedroom, Sara bent down and started to pull on her boots. Suddenly, someone entered the room. Sara looked up, startled. Olivia came in and closed the door behind her. She leaned against it, looking quite agitated.

"What's wrong?" asked Sara.

"Oh, Sara, I've really gone and done it this time."

Sara grinned. "Oh, good! What have you done?"

"I must be losing my senses! I can't think what Hetty is going to say. I haven't told her yet," moaned Olivia.

"Told her what?" pressed Sara.

Olivia took a deep breath. "I applied for that job at the *Chronicle*."

"You did!" yelped Sara. "Aunt Olivia, that's wonderful. Did you get it?"

"Well, not really. I'm sort of on trial. The only reason Mr. Tyler is trying me out is because I foolishly promised him..." Olivia looked miserable.

"What?" begged Sara, "What did you promise him?"

Olivia paused, and when she spoke the words poured out. "I told him I could find a photographer to come with me to help make the local stories more interesting." She flopped down on Sara's bed. "I'm in a fine mess, Sara."

"A photographer? Aunt Olivia, that's easy. You know who takes photographs."

Olivia looked stricken. "Sara, I realized coming home that I *cannot* ask Jasper to do this. He's so shy. He'd have to meet all sorts of people, and talk to them and oh, Sara, he'd absolutely hate it!"

Sara smiled. "He would do anything for you, Aunt Olivia. I'm sure of it."

"Sara, will you please stop all these nonsensical insinuations about Jasper and me!"

"You've always told me to tell the truth, haven't you?" prompted Sara. Olivia nodded. "Well, the truth is that Jasper Dale likes you. And I think the truth is that you like him, too."

Olivia said nothing, but Sara could tell her words had struck home.

"If you get changed right away, Aunt Olivia, we can go see Jasper on our way. What do you think?"

"I think I'm in a real pickle," confessed Olivia.

"I love pickles!" cried Sara, as Olivia hugged her.

It was still light as Sara and Olivia opened the gate to Golden Milestone. The sun, low in the hazy sky, warmed the rosy brick that faced the front of the modest, yet handsome, house. A light breeze, carrying just a tang of the nearby sea, tickled the lilac bushes guarding the walk. Olivia looked as light as the breeze herself, dressed as she was in a pretty white muslin dress, patterned with small clusters of dainty blue violets. Olivia raised her hand to Jasper Dale's door. She paused. She knocked. There was no answer, no sound. She bit her lip.

"He's not here, Sara. Let's go."

"Maybe he can't hear us," said Sara, rapping again, loudly.

"He's not here," repeated Olivia, looking relieved as she turned to go.

Sara opened the door and strolled in, calling, "Mr. Dale! It's Sara Stanley!"

Olivia wheeled round. "Sara! What are you doing?!" She made a dive for Sara's shoulder, but Sara was halfway down the hall.

"Mr. Dale? Mr. Dale? Are you home?" Olivia ran after Sara, who by now was in Jasper Dale's study!

"Oh, there you are!" trilled Sara, looking up at Jasper Dale.

Now, the reason Sara was looking up was that Jasper was looking down, from the second level of his study. He peered at her through his glasses, obviously startled to see her.

"G-Good day, Sara and..." Jasper looked quite faint. "Oh...and Miss K-King."

Jasper Dale's study was an inventive space, as you might imagine. There were two levels of bookshelves, connected by open wooden stairs, crammed with an amazing variety and number of volumes. On his cluttered desk was a globe and pinned up on a wall near the window was a map of the heavens, a map of Prince Edward Island and a photograph of the Great Pyramids of Egypt. A clothesline was strung across the room on which hung both photographs and socks.

Jasper started to descend the stairs, almost tripping halfway down.

Olivia was crimson. "Oh, Mr. Dale, I'm terribly sorry that we've intruded this way, obviously you're very busy and...Sara, we really must be going. We musn't be late for dinner."

"No!" said Jasper, more loudly than he meant to. "I mean, please, c-c-come in." He lifted piles of books from a couple of chairs, which he dusted off for his guests. "Excuse the..." Jasper gestured, somewhat vaguely, to the room.

"Oh, thank you, Mr. Dale," said Sara, sitting down.

Jasper looked at Olivia and smiled. There was that smile again, thought Sara. That special I-think-the-world-of-you smile. Olivia sat down. Jasper found himself standing awkwardly with an armful of books, gazing at Olivia.

"It's usually t-tidier, but Mrs. G-Griggs, the...uh, lady who...um..." Jasper put the books on the floor. They collapsed into a heap, which is just what Jasper wanted to do.

"Mrs. Griggs?" prompted Aunt Olivia.

"She's ill."

"Ah," replied Olivia, reaching down to retrieve a photograph that had escaped from the book pile.

"Thank you," mumbled Jasper, taking the photograph, "very much." A silence settled on the study.

"Mr. Dale," said Sara, finally, "I thought your library was in the barn."

"Oh...um...it was."

Another long pause developed. Sara and Aunt Olivia looked at each other. Sara and Aunt Olivia looked at Jasper Dale.

"But the—the m-mice were getting at the b-books. So..." He trailed off. Sara could see a question forming in his mind. "Is there...um...What can I do for you, Miss King?"

Ask him, ask him, Aunt Olivia, thought Sara, be brave!

Olivia looked down and examined the skirt of her dress.

"Well, actually, Jasper, I've come to ask a favor. But please feel free to just tell me directly if—if it's something you'd rather not do."

Jasper watched her, saying nothing.

"Aunt Olivia has a job at the newspaper," offered Sara gaily.

"Sara," warned Aunt Olivia.

Jasper brightened. "Oh, that's *good*, good—good for you."

"Well, I don't really," cautioned Aunt Olivia, "but I might, if..."

"If she can find a photographer," concluded Sara.

"Ah," said Jasper.

"Well," continued Olivia, "Sara just naturally thought of you. I know it's presumptuous of me, and it's all my fault for saying I'd do something when I really have no idea if I can even *write* the stories, let alone find someone to take photographs."

"I don't know how good my photographs would be, Miss King—" said Jasper.

"Please, call me Olivia."

Jasper continued. "I...um...it's just a hobby."

Olivia rose to go. "Well, your photographs would be much too good for Quentin Tyler. He really is the most aggravating man. He made me feel like a—like an absolute fool."

Jasper and Aunt Olivia's eyes locked briefly, for the first time in the entire conversation.

"Well, Olivia," said Jasper, "I don't know what kind of photographs you'll need, but I would be...um...pleased, yes, pleased to help you out in whatever way you can..." Jasper flushed. "I mean, in whatever way *I* can."

Sara suppressed a giggle. Olivia's pretty features melted into a smile.

"Thank you, Jasper."

Sara couldn't help smiling. Things were going just as she'd hoped!

Olivia moved towards the door. "Sara? We must be on our way. Sara? What are you daydreaming about?"

Jasper Dale looked surprisingly animated. "Oh, oh d-don't ask her, Olivia. She just might t-t-tell us. Then you'd never get to your dinner."

Aunt Olivia laughed merrily as Jasper saw them to the door.

"I'm only t-teasing you, Sara," Jasper assured Sara, as they all stepped out onto the porch.

Sara smiled. "I know that, Mr. Dale." He's perfect! she thought. After all, a person without a sense of humor was like a rainbow without a pot of gold—nice to look at, but disappointing in the end. Yes, Jasper Dale and Aunt Olivia were going to make a splendid couple, no doubt about it.

Chapter Eight

The gaslight bubbled low in the dining room, spreading a cheery glow that touched the china and crystal Aunt Janet had set out for the Grand

Occasion. There was a delicious roast of beef, with Aunt Hetty's special horseradish sauce; firm, tasty Prince Edward Island potatoes; turnip-carrot casserole made from a recipe Felicity had clipped from the Homemaker's Helper; a splendid jam roly-poly and, of course, Olivia's cinnamon buns, which were being saved "for later."

"I'm so full I swear I'll bust!" threatened Felix, pushing himself, finally, away from the table.

"Really, Felix," chided Felicity, "that's hardly an acceptable way to say that you've dined to the full."

Felix belched his reply.

"Excuse me," directed Hetty.

"Certainly," replied Felix cheerfully.

"Oh, Mother," howled Cecily, "can't we open the chest now? We've been waiting forever!"

With these words, it was as though a dam had burst. The children bounded from the dinner table and crowded round the chest, which had been brought into the parlor. Even the adults were excited, and Hetty's cheeks were unusually pink.

"Well," proclaimed Janet dramatically, as she leaned over the trunk, "the moment has finally arrived. Now, what have I done with the key?"

Felicity stamped her foot in frustration. "Oh, Mother, please!"

"Ma!" wailed Felix, adding to the din.

"Now, now," said Alec, in his quiet way. "Where would you have put the key, dear? Just think carefully, think back."

Sara realized she was holding her breath. Aunt Janet was a dear, but she could be somewhat scatter-brained.

"Oh!" squealed Aunt Janet, "here it is." She pulled a chain from inside the front of her dress, and sure enough, there was the key—sparkling, enticing. Hetty then stepped forward.

"Janet, I am the eldest, so it's my duty to open Aunt Arabella's chest."

"Well, Hetty, it has been under this roof for the past fifty years, and I think that gives me—"

"Oh, please," urged Sara, unable to contain herself another minute, "won't *someone* just open the chest?"

Aunt Janet slapped the key in Hetty's hand. Hetty reached down, placed the key in the old lock, and turned it. There was a distinct click. A ripple of excitement sprinted round the room. Alec reached over and lifted the creaky, heavy, wooden lid. Everyone pressed forward, straining to see what was in the trunk.

Hetty reached in and gently lifted a delicately embroidered white cotton cloth, which covered the contents of the chest.

"My, my," murmured Hetty, "look at the stitching

on that cloth, would you?" She handed the cloth to Janet, who placed it carefully on the chesterfield. Hetty reached farther down into the trunk and lifted out a lace petticoat. Clouds of fine dust burst into the air. Everyone started to cough. Hetty reached in again and pulled out a pair of disintegrating lace bloomers.

Felicity giggled. Sara smiled. Felix regarded the dusty items with disdain. "There ain't nothing in that trunk but dirty old clothes!"

"There must be other things in there," said Sara, "there simply *must* be!"

Olivia took over the unpacking from Hetty, who was coughing too much to enjoy the task. She shook out a long, ivory, satin dress, which hung in long, neglected shreds.

"Look," Olivia said sadly, "it's Arabella's wedding dress. Oh, what a shame."

"I'm afraid," said Hetty, "the moths have vandalized Aunt Arabella's entire trousseau. I'm sorry to say it, but the only place for this is the fire."

"I suppose you're right, Hetty," admitted Janet.

Olivia brought out another petticoat, two fine lace collars, and a lovely, long, pale-blue nightgown—all moth-eaten and useless. Everything in the trunk was beyond repair.

What was to have been the Grand Occasion was becoming a sad memorial to a past tragedy. Sara thought of Arabella as a young woman living in this very house, spending hours at her needlework, lovingly stitching her hopes and dreams into each item of clothing, each handsome set of pillowcases. And, in the evenings, her beloved Will would come to call and they would sit in the parlor, or out on the porch if the weather was fine, and talk softly about their wedding and their plans and about the ordinary comings and goings of their lives.

"Oh, look!" said Olivia, taking out a dark-green velvet case with an old gilt clasp. "Here are their photographs, Arabella and Will's."

Everyone crowded around and looked eagerly at the daguerreotypes in the old case.

"Why, Aunt Arabella wasn't a bit pretty!" exclaimed Felicity, disappointed.

"It's true," confirmed Aunt Janet, "but she had lovely color and a beautiful smile. I remember that smile."

"Will was terribly handsome," said Sara, examining the photographs closely before passing them to Cecily. There was something about Will's face, something Sara couldn't put her finger on. He vaguely reminded her of someone, but she couldn't think who.

"Aunt Arabella was too good for him," declared Hetty. "She should have looked beyond Avonlea for a husband. And the situation is the same today. There just aren't any real gentlemen in this town."

"Oh, I don't think that's true, Hetty," countered Olivia.

"What a terrible tragedy Will died so young," said Janet, gathering up the moth-eaten clothes.

Hetty looked severe. "Really, Janet, if that chest had been under my roof, I'd have broken the lock and aired it out years ago."

"Now, Hetty," cautioned Alec, "you know perfectly well that Arabella absolutely forbade us to open the chest until after her death."

Exactly, thought Sara. There *had* to be more in the trunk than Arabella's trousseau. There had to be something that needed protecting, "even unto death." Sara reached into the trunk. All that was left was a large mound of crumpled tissue paper in one corner. Sara lifted the yellowed paper.

"Look!" she cried, "a clock!" And sure enough, there was an ornate mantle clock, with tarnished gilt trim.

"Well, I never!" exclaimed Alec, as he held the clock up for everyone to see. "This clock used to sit on the fireplace mantle in Arabella's room. As a lad, I used to love to hear it chime."

"Well," sniffed Hetty, "it looks to me like it's beyond chiming now. Quite decrepit, I should say."

Sara examined the fine workmanship on the clock.

"It's still beautiful."

"Oh, really, Sara," snorted Felicity, "you can even see beauty in a rainy day!"

"Well," replied Sara serenely, "I would say rainy days are more interesting than beautiful. But I'm sure some can be beautiful, too. When I see one, I'll make sure to point it out to you, Felicity."

Janet moved towards the kitchen, carrying the old clothes.

"I don't suppose anyone's interested in a glass of punch and some of Aunt Olivia's cinnamon buns?"

"Are you kidding!" whooped Felix, as he led everyone into the kitchen.

As they all sipped their punch, Alec shoved all of Arabella's moth-eaten clothes into the kitchen stove. The flames licked the old garments, and then they were gone. The only things left were the photographs and the old clock, which stood in the center of the kitchen table. Sara pulled the clock towards her to examine it more closely.

Janet poured the last of the raspberry punch into Hetty's glass.

"Really, I shouldn't," said Hetty. "I always sleep dreadfully if I overindulge in your punch, Janet."

Janet smiled a little wickedly. "I know."

Sara reached for another cinnamon bun. She

knew she should stop eating, but they were just too, too delicious!

"Well," said Alec, lifting the clock upside down as he peered at it, "it pains me to say it, but I think this clock is just a piece of junk. There's really no use for it."

"I'll bet I know who could repair it," suggested Sara, looking pointedly at Olivia and thinking of Jasper Dale. Olivia shook her head.

"Nah," grumbled Felix. "There's no point spending any money fixing it. All the stuff in that trunk was just junk."

An unhappy look had settled on Felicity's fair features. "Well, the whole evening has been something of a disappointment," she said glumly.

"Except for Aunt Olivia's cinnamon buns," piped up Cecily, licking the last of the heavenly stickiness from her fingers.

"Thank you, Cecily, dear," said Olivia. "I thought the whole dinner was splendid, Janet."

"Uncle Alec," asked Sara, "could I have the clock? Please? Just to take home and look at?"

"Yes, by all means."

"I just can't stand to see everything that Aunt Arabella cared about thrown out."

"I know what you mean, Sara," said Olivia. "When I think of all the hopes and dreams Arabella packed away in that chest..."

"Oh, dear," teased Aunt Hetty, "I can just see it now. A new poem by Olivia J. King—'Hope's End.'"

"Really, Hetty," said Olivia, helping Sara lift the clock. "Sara, let's put this in the front hall so we won't forget it on our way out." "Oh, I won't forget it," Sara assured Olivia as they left the kitchen.

When they came back down the hall, Sara could hear Felix, Cecily and Felicity in the parlor with their father, talking over the events of the evening. Janet and Hetty were alone in the kitchen, washing up the punch glasses, and their conversation floated out into the hall. It was one of those odd moments. Entering the kitchen would have stopped the conversation, but Sara and Olivia found themselves overhearing it, almost before they realized what was happening.

"But Hetty," argued Janet, "Olivia's getting some recognition and—I'm going to say it, Hetty—I think it's wonderful."

"Recognition, pish-posh," replied Hetty. "She's accomplished nothing of note. Oh, believe me, Janet, Olivia gives me great cause for concern—mooning about, scribbling away. Thank goodness most of us have Grandfather King's get-up-and-go."

"Well, then," declared Janet, "I should think you would be pleased that Olivia doesn't want to stray too much. You'd be lost without her."

"Me!" exclaimed Hetty. "Oh, dear no. She'd be lost without me, I'm afraid."

There was a little pause. "I remember when Olivia and Edwin Clarke were engaged," remarked Janet. "You were very upset, Hetty, and don't you deny it."

"Well of course I was upset! Edwin Clarke wasn't suitable for Olivia, wasn't suitable at all. Olivia made the proper decision, breaking off their engagement."

"All I'm saying, Hetty, is that I think you would miss Olivia terribly if she left Rose Cottage."

"Olivia is just a child, Janet, in many ways. I can't see her up and leaving, although she has been acting rather strangely lately."

There was another silence, broken only by the tinkle of the punch glasses as Hetty placed them carefully on the counter. Sara looked at her Aunt Olivia. Clearly, Aunt Hetty's remarks had hurt her feelings.

"You'll show her," whispered Sara, "you'll see."

Olivia said nothing, and was very quiet on the walk home.

That night Sara had trouble getting to sleep. She had to admit this was probably because of an excess of cinnamon buns, plus three Cupids. She lay in bed and looked out at the millions of stars winking in the great, blue night sky. When she was a very little girl, her father had told her that each star was an angel who had been lost, but who had finally found a home in the heavens. Maybe Aunt Arabella and Will were up there, together, radiant, shining for all the world to see. Sara snuggled down and finally slept, peacefully, lulled by the warm breeze of the Avonlea night.

Chapter Nine

It was as if, overnight, spring had been stolen. Sara looked out the next morning at the trees swaying and creaking in the wind, their anxious arms tapping against her bedroom window. Rain sliced the dark, roiling sky and, in the distance, Sara could hear the screams of seagulls and the rumbling ocean surging against the shore. To add to all this, Sara didn't feel at all well. Apparently, the Grand Occasion of the night before had been a bit too grand for Sara's stomach. She groaned. Never again would she eat so much, she vowed to herself. Now she would have to go downstairs and face Aunt Hetty and ask to stay home from school. Aunt Hetty wouldn't be pleased. Sara lay back in bed and closed her eyes.

Hetty clanged the coffeepot down on the stove. She wheeled on Olivia.

"I have never heard such nonsense, Olivia. Taking employment at a—a newspaper. No proper King woman has ever done such a thing, thank goodness."

Olivia cut her toast with determination. "Hetty, no King woman was a teacher before you, and *you've* made a success of it."

"That's entirely different. I'm the eldest. It was, it *is*, my duty to provide for you."

Olivia took a bite of toast. "I don't want to be provided for, Hetty. I can take care of myself."

Hetty raised an eyebrow. "Well, that remains to be seen, doesn't it? And don't talk with your mouth full, if you please."

Much to her own surprise, Olivia's fist came down on the table, causing the sugar bowl to jump nervously.

"I am not a child, Hetty! And I don't appreciate being spoken to as one."

"I'm sorry," muttered Hetty, stiffly.

Olivia's voice softened. "Hetty, try to understand. You have your teaching and Janet has her family, and I need to do something in my own right. You've said it yourself. I don't see why you're protesting so much."

Aunt Hetty turned a bit red. "I'm not protesting.

It *is* about time you did something, but..." She turned away from Olivia and looked out the window at the bending trees.

"But what?" pressed Olivia.

"Very well," said Hetty, a tone of exasperation lacing her voice. "Go ahead, do what you will, any way the wind blows. Next thing you know, you'll be flitting off like—like Ruth."

"Sara's mother didn't flit off, Hetty. She fell in love and moved away."

Hetty sniffed. "Same thing."

"Hetty," said Olivia, "I am not going to flit off." With that, she turned to leave the kitchen. She almost bumped into Sara, who had finally found the strength to come downstairs. Sara crept to the table and sat down.

"Good heavens, child," exclaimed Hetty, "you look as white as a ghost. Whatever's the matter?"

"Oh, Aunt Hetty, I feel so horrible," wailed Sara. "My stomach is rolling around like a lost soul!"

"Oh, dear," said Aunt Hetty, "too much of Aunt Janet's dinner." Olivia nodded in sympathy. Hetty patted Sara gently on the back. "There, there, child. No school for you today."

Sara looked up. "Really?" She felt somewhat better already. It was amazing.

"No, indeed," confirmed Hetty. "Today you'll

stay in bed and have beef tea every three hours. That should bring you round nicely."

"But I hate beef tea," moaned Sara.

Hetty started to collect her books for school. "And if you're feeling better later, Sara, perhaps you might move Aunt Arabella's clock out of the hallway outside your door. I tripped over it twice this morning. Someone could take a nasty tumble, you know."

Sara moaned again.

"Oh, dear," said Olivia, "you really do need that beef tea. I'll make up a whole pot of it before I go out this afternoon."

Hetty looked out at the rain and started searching for her umbrella. "And where are you off to this afternoon, Olivia?"

"Well, actually, I have quite a list of places to go, for the newspaper." Olivia smiled slightly. "Jasper Dale's picking me up at one o'clock."

Hetty froze. Oh, oh, thought Sara. Aunt Olivia had omitted telling Aunt Hetty this one little detail.

"Jasper Dale?" Hetty croaked.

"He's taking photographs for me," said Olivia cheerfully, "I suppose you could say we're going to be something of a team. Now, if you'll excuse me, Hetty, I must go to the pantry and get that beef tea for Sara." She sailed out of the kitchen.

❧❧❧

"Look," Olivia said sadly, "it's Arabella's wedding dress. Oh, what a shame."

"I'm afraid," said Hetty, "the moths have vandalized Aunt Arabella's entire trusseau. I'm sorry to say it, but the only place for this is the fire."

❦❦❦

"Mr. Tyler, surely you don't believe that
nothing ever happens in Avonlea?"

"The only excitement I have is with my bank manager,
who is very unhappy about my overdraft.
Miss King, I've inherited a — a dead horse."

cxcxcxc

Jasper carefully removed the back of the clock and
reached in. "Wait — wait — no, I don't th–think —
yes, there is something in here."
Sara's eyes widened. "I knew it! I just knew it!"

Aunt Hetty shot Sara a look. "Did you know all about this, Sara?"

"Well, no, not all about it."

Hetty jammed on her hat. "You two!" she complained as she opened the door, snapped her black umbrella open and journeyed out into the rain.

Sara sat at the kitchen table, reluctantly sipping her beef tea and leafing through the most recent copy of her favourite magazine, *Leisure Hours*. What a delicious problem, deciding which new story to read first. Topsy sat curled in Sara's lap, warmly dozing and twitching.

Olivia placed a large bowl of tapioca pudding on the window sill to cool. She smiled at Sara. "Feeling better?"

"Yes, thank you." And she was, too. She hated to admit it might have been the beef tea, but whatever it was, her stomach had, in fact, stopped spinning.

Olivia looked out the window. "Look, Sara, I think the sun's breaking through."

Sara set Topsy down and got up from the table, and joined Aunt Olivia at the window. Topsy looked deeply offended and dropped to the floor with a dramatic thud. Sure enough, the dark clouds were scudding away, leaving the sun confidently spreading its radiance on the world. And a very pretty world it was, too, a dripping chandelier of raindrops lit by the sun's rays.

"Aunt Olivia," said Sara, "I was wondering, since I'm feeling ever so much better, if I could come along with you and Mr. Dale this afternoon? I mean, to help out. I'd be very good, and I could be your assistant!"

Aunt Olivia considered this.

"I don't know, Sara. You still look peaky, and I don't think Aunt Hetty would approve."

"Oh, I think she would," replied Sara. "After all, being a reporter's assistant would be a truly educational experience."

Olivia smiled. "You're sure you're feeling better now? Really?"

"Cross my heart," Sara assured Olivia fervently.

"And out of all the things in the chest, Mr. Dale, the only thing worth keeping was Aunt Arabella's clock! Now what do you think of that?" Sara was sitting between Aunt Olivia and Jasper, bouncing up and down like a peanut on the seat of the buggy.

"I—I'm sure I don't know, Sara," replied Jasper, guiding the horse around a large puddle of water in the middle of the road. The buggy leaned to one side. Olivia held on to Sara with one hand and her hat with the other. She laughed merrily.

"Oh, dear, Jasper, perhaps we should have left this until tomorrow, when the roads had dried somewhat."

"Not a b-bit of it, Olivia," said Jasper, firmly. "You are about to launch your career as a reporter for the Avonlea *Chronicle*, and not a moment too soon."

Sara realized that she'd never heard Jasper Dale say so many words without stumbling. She also realized she'd never seen Jasper in a suit, except in her dreams, of course. He actually looked better in real life. And, Sara realized, she had stopped thinking of him as the Awkward Man.

"But there's still something missing," mused Sara. "Old clothes aren't enough of a reason to absolutely forbid anyone from going through that trunk. I'm going to take another look in it. I'm going to examine it inch by inch."

"You-you're just determined to find something, aren't you, Sara? Maybe Avonlea has its own Sherlock Holmes," teased Jasper.

"Its own *Shirley* Holmes!" replied Sara, and they all laughed as they jogged along in the sunshine, with Jasper's mare, Dolly, splashing bravely through the mud.

"Aunt Olivia, what's our first port of call?" asked Sara as they rounded a lazy curve in the road. By now it was a full, welcoming spring day; the wind and rain now had been safely blown out to the great Atlantic.

Aunt Olivia consulted a small black notebook. "The Hendersons. Mrs. Henderson's daughter is getting married."

Sara's eyes lit up. "Which daughter?"

"Good q-question," added Jasper. "The Hendersons have a...um...c-cartload of daughters."

"The bride-to-be is Bessie, the eldest."

Sara clapped her hands together. "Oh, I *love* weddings! Don't you love weddings, Mr. Dale?"

Olivia gave Sara a little nudge with her elbow, which Sara blithely ignored.

Jasper seemed to be watching the road especially intently.

"I...um...a wedding is all right, I suppose, if—if you're the m-m-marrying kind."

Aunt Olivia burst out laughing. "Oh, Jasper, that's funny!" Jasper looked a little hurt. "No, really," said Olivia. Jasper looked a little pleased.

Sara persisted. "Aunt Olivia, don't you think weddings are just the grandest things?"

"Well, Sara, I think if two people want to get married, weddings make a lot of sense."

Jasper didn't laugh, but he smiled that special smile at Olivia.

"Well," confided Sara gravely, "when I get married I want to be outdoors, in a lovely wooded glen. And I'd like a dress made out of clouds, with stars for buttons and a garland of moonbeams in my hair."

"That's a very romantic picture, Sara," Olivia observed softly.

"And there would be so much love there, in those woods, that everyone and everything would be touched by it—like a sheen of silver. And the love would last forever."

Sara's words had spun out a strange kind of web, and nothing more was said until they turned into the Hendersons' lane.

In the parlor, Mrs. Henderson regarded her daughter with alarm. "Now then, what kind of a smile is that? You should be happy, my girl. You're going to be in the newspaper."

Bessie shifted uncomfortably on the sofa. "Mr. Dale's not ready to take the photograph yet, Mother," she whispered.

And this was quite true. Jasper was in the process of setting his heavy camera atop the sturdy wooden tripod. Sara stood by, holding the black cloth that would block out all light, making the photographic print possible.

"Have you made your own wedding dress, Bessie?" Aunt Olivia asked, her notebook at the ready.

"Well, of course she has," replied Mrs. Henderson indignantly. "My Bessie is very handy with a needle, very handy indeed."

Jasper did a final adjustment on his camera, and peered through the lens. "M-Miss H-H-Henderson, I—I—"

"What is it, Jasper?" snapped Mrs. Henderson. "Are you ready to take our photograph, is that what you're trying to say?"

"N-N-Not yet," sputtered Jasper, miserably. Sara handed him the black cloth and smiled encouragingly.

"Mr. Dale is a very good photographer, Mrs. Henderson," said Olivia evenly, "He'll be the one to decide when it's time to take the photograph."

Mrs. Henderson acknowledged this brusquely and joined Bessie on the sofa.

"Tell me, Bessie," said Olivia, "when is the wedding to be?"

Bessie opened her mouth to answer, but she wasn't quick enough. Her mother leapt in. "Oh, as soon as we can arrange it. I feel sure that Bessie's engagement picture in the *Chronicle*, along with the announcement, will be just the thing to spur Clem on to name a date."

"You haven't set a date yet?!" Sara said with alarm.

"Well, he's a McLeod, you know, and the

McLeods are something *awful* at putting things off."

"Oh, dear," said Aunt Olivia, in a somewhat muted voice.

Mrs. Henderson focused in on Sara. "And aren't you supposed to be in school, Sara Stanley?"

"Yes. No! I mean I'm sick. I mean, I *was* sick."

Mrs. Henderson's thin lips pursed together until they finally disappeared altogether. Jasper flung the black cloth over his head and the camera.

"If y-you...um...could you j-just smile now, Bessie?"

"Well, of course she can smile, can't you?" prompted Mrs. Henderson. "Don't grimace, girl— smile!"

There was a loud "pop," a brilliant flash, and the deed was done.

"What a dreadful woman that Mrs. Henderson is!" exclaimed Sara as they trotted down the lane and back onto the muddy road. "She didn't let poor Bessie say a word. I wanted to throttle her."

"No wonder Bessie's finally getting married," reflected Olivia. "Can you imagine living with *that* every day?"

Jasper spoke quietly. "S-Sometimes we forget how unkind p-people can be t-to each other. K-Kindness should be a simple thing, freely g-given."

Olivia looked at Jasper quite tenderly.

"Aunt Hetty always says that most people treat their animals with more kindness than they do their families," confirmed Sara. "Speaking of which, next stop, Pat Frewen and his prize pig, right, Aunt Olivia?"

"Right you are, Sara. Right you are."

Pat Frewen held up a huge, red rosette with "First Prize" stamped on it in loud gold letters.

"Yup," he assured them, "first prize at the Charlottetown Fair for my beauty, Zachariah."

Mr. Pat Frewen was a jolly, apple-cheeked, middle-aged bachelor, who was an enthusiastic and expert pig farmer. He wasn't a well-educated man but, unlike Mrs. Henderson, he had a natural warmth of spirit and a great generosity toward his fellow creatures, human or animal. So it was something of a sadness to Pat that at age forty-four, he still hadn't found a woman to share his life. Like many people, Pat Brewen hid his sadness by making jokes about his unwed position.

"Now, Miss King," mourned Pat, as they all tramped through the large, well-tended barn, "don't tell me you still ain't hitched?"

Olivia turned pink. "Well, no, Pat."

"And you such a pretty thing, it don't seem right. It don't seem right at all. I'd make you a Missus in a minute!"

Olivia turned pinker.

"And what about you, Mr. Dale?" pressed Pat. "You're a bit of an odd duck, ain't you? Just like me, I guess, no woman in her right mind will have you."

"I—I guess n-not, Pat," mumbled Jasper.

"And as for you, Miss Stanley, I bet you're already breaking the boys' hearts, ain't you?"

"Oh, most of the boys in Avonlea aren't my type, Mr. Brewen," replied Sara, rather haughtily.

"Ain't your type, ain't your type," he repeated fondly, chuckling and shaking his head. "No offence now, Miss Stanley, but I think maybe you should wait a few years before you get your types all set up!" Olivia and Jasper laughed too, which made Sara a bit cross.

They rounded a corner, and Pat stopped in front of a large stall. He spread open his thick arms and paused dramatically.

"There he be, folks. Zachariah. Weighs in at two hundred and twenty-six pounds. None of them others even came close, did they?"

As Aunt Olivia made notes and Jasper set up his equipment, Pat squatted down and scratched Zachariah's ears. The large hog looked up, grunting appreciatively.

"Zach, you and me are gonna have our picture in the paper, isn't that just the darndest thing?"

"N-Now, Pat," stammered Jasper, "if you could

just get Zachariah's head up, looking at the camera—
j-j-ust like that—good—steady as she goes—"

Pat Brewen was grinning from ear to ear as the
flash went off. But poor Zachariah! The bright flash
sent him into a panic, and he bolted from the stall,
squealing injustice to the very rafters! Pat raced
after him.

"Darn pig!! You come back here, or I'll turn you
into a side of bacon before you can say 'Good morning'! You're no first prize. You come back here,
Zachariah Brewen!!"

Olivia and Sara were still laughing as they
walked back towards the buggy, while Jasper shook
his head.

"This should give you some good m-m-material
for your stories, Olivia. Mr. T-T-Tyler won't have
any excuse not to hire you."

Olivia smiled tentatively. "Oh, I hope you're
right, Jasper."

"Of course he's right," confirmed Sara, as Jasper
courteously extended his hand to her. "Thank you,
kind sir," she said, feeling quite grown up as they
trotted down the muddy lane.

Chapter Ten

Sara had persuaded Olivia to drop her at the King Farm, promising that she would be home before Hetty got back from school. It was all working out perfectly! Sara would get another chance to inspect the blue chest, while Olivia and Jasper would have some time alone.

Felicity expertly rolled out some cookie dough. "I thought you were supposed to be sick today, Sara Stanley."

"I was. But I'm much better now. I bet I didn't miss anything in school, anyway."

"As a matter of fact, we studied a lovely poem, by Keats. And Sally Potts read it beautifully, quite beautifully."

"As well as *I* would have?" challenged Sara, who was very proud of her reading abilities.

Felicity reached for her cookie cutter. "Well..." She wasn't going to give in, unless she absolutely had to.

Sara took a deep breath. "Felicity, what's that heavenly smell?"

"I've got a blackberry pie in the oven. And do you know what, Sara?"

"What?"

"I had a bit of extra pastry left over so I made a

"K" to decorate the top of the pie. "K" for King. Wasn't that imaginative of me?"

Sara was saved from having to respond, because just then Felix burst into the kitchen, slamming the door behind him. He grabbed a blob of raw cookie dough and plunked himself down on a kitchen chair.

"I've been thinking," said Sara.

"Well, hallelujah!" bellowed Felix.

Felicity swatted Felix with a wooden baking spoon. "Stop eating my cookie dough, Felix, I mean it! And don't make such an uproar!"

Felix grinned. "Your cookie dough is the best in the whole universe, Felicity. I swear—the best." Felicity relented, slightly.

Sara walked over to the blue chest, an intense look on her face.

"I wonder what was really in here, what was so important to Arabella? What?"

Felicity sighed. "We've been through this, Sara. It was her wedding dress. She couldn't bear the thought of anyone else seeing it."

"No! It had to be something more important than her wedding dress."

"For goodness sake, nothing's more important than your very own wedding dress, especially if you never got to wear it because your fiancé shot himself!"

Felix's eyes glinted. "That's what I'm interested

in—murder dark and evil. All this stuff about dresses is just sissy."

"It wasn't murder, Felix," corrected Felicity. "Mother said it was thought to be suicide."

"Mother doesn't know everything," Felix replied boldly.

Sara lifted the lid of the trunk. "There *must* be something else in here."

Felicity looked exasperated. "Really, Sara, you're never satisfied to let a story stop where it should stop. You're always letting your imagination run away with you."

Sara peered intently at the trunk, trying to see right through it, right into the very wood. She remembered reading a story in *Leisure Hours* about Malveen the Magnificent, a great magician, who had advised, "Sometimes mysteries are seen more clearly with eyes closed." Sara stepped back from the chest and scrunched her eyes tightly shut. She concentrated, every muscle tensed.

"Look, Sara's fallen asleep standing up," laughed Felix. "I thought only horses could do that."

"Shhhh," instructed Felicity, "let her think."

As Sara stood there, eyes shut tight, she started having an odd sensation. It wasn't that she "saw" an image or picture, but she started feeling drawn towards the trunk. She took a step towards it, slowly, like a sleepwalker, her eyes still closed. She

took another step. The silence in the kitchen crack-
led all around her. Then she opened her eyes and
hopped into the open trunk!

"Sara!" shrieked Felicity, "what are you doing?"

Felix started to laugh. "Hey, let's close the lid
and open it in fifty years!"

Sara knelt down, again closing her eyes. She put
one hand on the bottom of the trunk and the other
over the edge, flat on the kitchen floor. Yes! There
was no question about it!

"Look! The trunk is shallower on the inside than
it is on the outside!"

"I don't understand," said Felicity.

Sara stood up. "See?" She spread her arms tri-
umphantly. "It's got a—" The end of Sara's sentence
was cut off by a loud splintering noise, which was,
in fact, Sara crashing through the bottom of the
trunk. Felicity and Felix rushed over to rescue their
cousin. Sara popped up, grinning.

"It's got a false bottom. I knew it!" She clam-
bered out of the trunk, and the three children
looked at each other, wide-eyed.

Felicity peered into the trunk. "Maybe there are
jewels!"

"Or treasure—or coins," shouted Felix. "We'll
be rich!" He started to jump up and down in a
dance of joy. "Rich! I'll be able to buy that red fire
truck from Eaton's catalogue! Rich!!"

Sara reached into the trunk and carefully removed pieces of jagged wood, searching for what might be underneath. There was nothing there—no leather jewel case, no glinting emeralds and rubies, no shining gold coins.

Felicity looked disappointed. "There's nothing there. It's all over." She trudged back to her cookie dough. Felix turned away, as visions of the fire truck raced off.

"No, wait," whispered Sara. She groped into a far corner. Something was there! Sara lifted out a package of yellowed envelopes, tied with a faded pink ribbon. "Look!"

"Letters," snorted Felix. "Just a bunch of stupid letters." Felicity agreed. What a disappointment Aunt Arabella's trunk had turned out to be.

Felix walked toward the door. There were more interesting things to do outside. He paused.

"Felicity, something's burning!"

Felicity looked alarmed as she bounded to the stove. She grabbed a tea towel, opened the oven door and rescued the blackberry pie.

"Oh, why did I forget to watch it? That stupid trunk!" Felicity was almost in tears. "And that was the last of this year's preserves!"

The faded packet of letters was warm in Sara's hands—almost alive. Sara felt that Arabella was about to speak, from across the years. She hugged the letters close.

"Felicity, do you think your mother would mind if I took these home to have a look at?"

Felicity was involved in mourning her blackberry pie.

"Of course not. Take them. Oh, my poor pie."

Sara stood up and carefully slipped the letters in the pocket of her pinafore. Suddenly, she had a splendid idea. A wonderful thought! She looked at the blackberry pie, which was really only well done, not burnt. Felicity *was* rather inclined to take a tragic view of her cooking failures.

"Felicity, I love burned blackberry pie. Why don't you let me take this disaster home—remove it before it becomes a painful reminder to you?"

Felicity brightened somewhat. "Oh, would you, Sara? I just can't face mother right now. Those were the last of this year's preserves," she repeated, wistfully.

"So you said," replied Sara sympathetically as Felicity wrapped the pie in a pretty blue-and-white tea towel.

Now, thought Sara as she said her goodbyes, just one little stop on the way home. Just one little stop and the day would turn out quite splendidly. Quite splendidly, indeed.

There was no sign of Jasper Dale as Sara stealthily opened the gate and walked up the path to the front door of Golden Milestone. A strange thrill rippled down her spine. It was one thing to call out for Jasper, hoping he was there. It was quite another to pray, please, oh please, that he wasn't home. This was trespassing, no doubt about it.

Sara slowly mounted the steps to the white, wooden veranda, wincing at each creak and crack under her feet. To one side of the screen door was a small table. Sara carefully set the blackberry pie down on it. She smiled to herself. With the telltale "K" on it, Jasper couldn't think the gift was from anyone other than his beloved Olivia King.

Sara was about to go back down the steps when a thought sprang into her mind. Yes! She could open the door, enter the house, go up the stairs to the secret room, the mysterious room Mrs. Griggs had talked about. Sara could see with her own eyes what was really in there. She reached out to the screen door. Jumping Jehoshaphat, as Felix would say, what on earth was she doing? This was *someone else's house*, for goodness sake! With an involuntary gasp Sara spun round, clattered down the veranda steps, burst through the garden gate, raced down the lane and sped onto the road. She ran, in a panic, until she was out of breath and almost home.

Hetty looked skeptical. "Well, Sara, if you started feeling better around noon, you really should have come to school for the half day. We did the seven-times multiplication tables this afternoon."

"You're right," admitted Sara. "But Aunt Olivia thought it would be educational to help her and Jasper with their newspaper stories."

"Mr. Dale to you, Sara," Hetty corrected. "You must show respect for your elders."

Olivia started to set the table. "Oh, Sara's just high-spirited, Hetty. Rather like you as a girl."

Sara could feel the letters in her pocket, calling to her. She was dying to read them.

"Whatever do you mean, Olivia? I was never rude, and presuming to call someone by their Christian name is quite untoward."

Sara desperately wanted to get up to her room, close the door and plunge into Arabella's love letters. She sidled towards the door.

"Sara, where are you off to?" demanded Hetty. "We have plenty of time before supper to go over the multiplication tables."

Sara clutched her stomach. "I'm starting to have a stomach-ache again, Aunt Hetty."

"Sara, I hope that's not a fib."

"Really it's not, Aunt Hetty." One more minute

of this and it *will* be the truth, thought Sara. "I think I should go up to my room."

"Sara was a great help to us today, Hetty," Olivia added. "It wouldn't hurt her to rest a bit."

Hetty agreed. "I'm not an ogre, you know. It's just that you seemed recovered and now you say you're ill again! At any rate, it's more beef tea for you, Sara. Olivia will bring it up to you. Now off you go."

"Thank you, Aunt Hetty. You're wonderful."

"Don't be silly," said Hetty, pleased. "Up to your room now."

Outside Sara's window, the goldfinches had started their evening calls, serenading the fading lemon sun. Soon, the murmuring softness of twilight would settle on Avonlea with all her mysteries, past and present.

Sara sat up in bed, her heart hammering in anticipation as she unknotted the flattened pink ribbon that bound the yellowed letters. Arabella herself had last touched that ribbon, thought Sara, on a sad morning long ago. But long ago seemed right now as Sara opened the first envelope and pulled out a fine, cream-colored sheet inscribed with even, black script. She settled back on her pillows. Sara read:

February 1, 1851

My dearest, darling Arabella,

I am happy today in a way I've never been happy before. I still can't believe that you're going to be my wife and that, together, we will weave our lives together in a tapestry that will be ours to create. I know it's the same old world as it was yesterday, but it feels new to me, and I thank you for that, my darling. I tell myself that April 29th isn't so very far away, and with all the wedding plans we have to make I can only hope the days speed by. I'm sure they will. I suspect that sitting down with our mothers and deciding on a guest list will take up many an evening!

I love you, Arabella, and whatever the future may bring, my love for you will burn bright. Know that always.

Forever,
Your Will.

Sara put down the letter. Her eyes brimmed with tender tears. Poor Will! Poor Arabella! What a happy couple they would have been. I hope that someday, thought Sara, someone will write a love letter like that to me. She sniffled. And if only Jasper would write that kind of a letter to Aunt Olivia, then they could weave a wonderful life together, Sara felt sure of it. A life full of hope and looking to a happy future. That was the thing, Will sounded so full of hope and life. The letter didn't sound the least bit like it was written by someone who was going to kill himself.

Sara reached down for another letter, but as she did so, something heavier fell away from the bottom of the packet. Sara picked up a slender, red, leather diary. She opened it. Arabella's diary! She read the first entry, written in graceful, flowing script.

January 1, 1851

Well, it's a New Year, and I am filled with joy, for I feel it will be a happy year for me. It's true, I'm so in love, it almost makes me dizzy! I go through the days doing normal things, eating and baking and going for walks and helping my aunt with the house-keeping, but underneath is a bubbling spring of pure happiness, which can over-flow at any moment.

I've made up my mind that if Will asks me to marry him, I'll accept. What am I talking about! I couldn't possibly say no—it would break my heart, forever. He is just the dearest soul, quick and funny and handsome, and he just seems to love me for who I am. I think this is a rare gift, for I see so many couples who think, "Oh, if so-and-so could just change, then things would be perfect." And it never happens. And I love my Will just the way he is. He's in Charlottetown right now, sorting out some complicated affairs to do with his family's business, but he writes me every day, and I almost run to the post office to pick up his letters!

I'm going out for a walk now. It's a lovely, still winter evening, and a full moon is casting her diamond light on the snows of Avonlea. I want to gaze up at that dear old moon and think of Will, looking up to the very same heavens.

Sara wanted terribly to race ahead in Arabella's diary to the awful events of her wedding day and the day after, but she decided that she owed Arabella and Will the courtesy of reading the diaries and the letters in sequence. That way, Sara could get a real feeling for their romance, and the way events had actually unfolded for the star-crossed lovers. She must, as Aunt Hetty would say, "exercise restraint."

Sara walked to the window. The twilight would

have a calming effect on her—clear her mind. Sara gazed out the window and gasped. Jasper Dale was coming up the walk! What was he doing here?! He was supposed to be at home, eating what he thought was Aunt Olivia's blackberry pie, silently pleased, but too shy to respond. Didn't Jasper understand?! He was supposed to be too awkward to come and say thank you. But there he was, almost on the front steps, grasping a bouquet of mayflowers in one hand and a book in the other!

Sara quickly slipped the letters and the diary under her pillow and flew down the stairs. She had to stop him from saying anything! She had to stop Aunt Olivia from finding out she'd been playing Cupid!

Before Jasper could even knock on the door, Sara flung it open. Her words tumbled out like a troupe of circus acrobats.

"Oh hello there Jasper what beautiful flowers I'll make sure Aunt Olivia gets them and the book too, yes, I'll make sure she gets that too, goodnight!" She was about to close the door on a startled Jasper Dale when Olivia came into the hall.

"Sara, what's going on?"

"Oh, it's nothing, Aunt Olivia. Some kind of delivery for you, I'm taking care of it." But Olivia was at the door.

"Jasper! How lovely to see you."

Oh no, thought Sara, as she shrank into a corner, it's all over. I'm finished. I'll be found out, humiliated, oh, I've got to do something! But what?!

Jasper offered the fragrant bouquet to Olivia. "I—I just want t-to thank you for—for—"

Olivia beamed. "Oh, that's not necessary, Jasper. I enjoyed the day just as much as you did, I'm sure."

Jasper held out the book. "Please—I—I—found this—it's about pigs. F-F-For your article. For background."

Sara felt hot and dizzy. She leaned against the wall for support. Aunt Hetty came out from the kitchen, curious as to who their visitor was. Sara's mind was churning. She had to do something!

"Oh, it's you, Jasper."

"Good evening, H-H-Hetty, I just wanted t- t-to, it's about the p-p—"

Sara gave a piteous cry and slumped to the floor in a dead faint. Well, of course, Hetty and Olivia and Jasper all rushed to her aid, patting her cheeks and fanning her face. As Sara had anticipated, Hetty took charge.

"Olivia, run up to my room and get my smelling salts from the top drawer of the bureau. Quickly! Jasper, I think it's best if you leave us now. We'll attend to Sara."

Sara opened her eyes just the tiniest slit. Jasper was turning to go.

"If—if there's anything I can—"

"Thank you, Jasper. But we're quite all right. It's best you be on your way."

Olivia raced down the stairs with the smelling salts just as Jasper was closing the door. Sara let out a enormous sigh of relief. Hetty stroked Sara's face.

"Oh, she's coming round! Oh, thank heavens. Oh, Sara, you gave us quite a turn, didn't she, Olivia?"

The Aunts helped Sara to her room and put a cool cloth on her forehead and tucked her in and brought beef tea and decided to wait until tomorrow to see about calling a doctor. And they let Topsy sleep on Sara's bed just this one night, and they were so lovingly concerned that Sara felt quite guilty. But not too guilty because, as one poet said, "Desperate times call for desperate measures."

Later, when the house was hushed and still, Sara lit her lamp, ate three Cupids and read Arabella's letters and diary far into the night. They were wonderful and romantic, but it had been a long day. Before she could finish the letters, and quite against her will, Sara's eyes became heavy.

She slept restlessly, dreaming of Will and Arabella getting married in Jasper's secret room, which seemed to be at the bottom of a bottle-green ocean. She dreamt, too, of Aunt Hetty cutting out cookies in the shape of a "K." Aunt Hetty looked darkly at Sara as she put them in the oven and even more darkly as she took them out, burned to a crisp.

Chapter Eleven

The next morning, Sara woke late. It was almost eleven o'clock, and the day was well on its way. Propped up on Sara's dresser was a note written in Hetty's distinct, authoritative handwriting.

Dear Sara,
     Aunt Olivia and I decided that the best course of action this morning was to let you sleep as long as you could. Sleep is a great healer. I am at school, of course, and Olivia will be back around noon. I've left a fresh pot of beef tea which you must drink. Please do not disobey me in this, Sara. You are obviously suffering some kind of malady, and if you aren't feeling better by this evening, we will have to call the doctor in. So rest is the order of the day. I'll see you after school.

                                        Aunt Hetty

Next to Aunt Hetty's note was one from Aunt Olivia, written in haste, judging from the sprightly dashes and loops scrawled across the page.

Dear Sara—I hope you're feeling better this morning! You gave us an awful scare last night, you dear girl. I'm off in a minute to drop off my stories to Mr. Tyler at the *Chronicle*. I'm so nervous, I feel quite light-headed! I'll tell you all about it when I get back. Now, you just rest this morning, dear. And the beef tea isn't <u>too</u> bad, I drank a bit of it myself this morning, to settle my nerves. Oh, wish me luck, Sara.

Love,
Aunt Olivia

Sara indeed wished Aunt Olivia all the luck in the world, with all her might, as she padded down to the kitchen. She dutifully brought a cup of beef tea back upstairs. She sipped it as she curled up with Topsy to finish reading the last of Arabella's letters and diary.

Olivia clenched the large manila envelope in her perspiring hands as the buggy jogged along main street. Why, oh, why had she allowed this to happen? She really must look more carefully into the King genealogy. Clearly, there was a nest of insanity lodged in some branch of the family tree. And the incredible thing was that everyone else looked normal as they went about their morning business. Mrs. Lawson waved a cheery "hello" and Reverend Leonard politely tipped his hat as he turned into the post office. Sitting beside Olivia, Jasper looked almost *happy*. Of course, his photographs were awfully good, Olivia thought. Much better than her writing.

"Well," said Jasper, swinging down from the buggy and offering Olivia his hand, "here we go." He tied Dolly's reins to the hitching post in front of the *Chronicle*'s offices.

Olivia bit her lip as she straightened her straw hat. "Jasper, would you—I mean, would it be all right if I went in alone? I'm not trying to be rude, but..."

Jasper was understanding. "I'll be waiting right here, Olivia. You can count on it."

"Oh, you're a dear!" exclaimed Olivia, surprised that the words just popped out of her mouth. She really was discombobulated today! Jasper reddened, but didn't look away. He took Olivia's hand and spoke softly.

"Good luck, Olivia."

Unable to respond because her mouth was so dry, Olivia squared her shoulders and vanished into the newspaper office.

Once in the door, she almost collided with Mr. Hyde, the bank manager, who was just nearing the end of remarks, directed, with considerable heat, at Quentin Tyler.

"You heard me, Mr. Tyler. I told you last week and I'm telling you again! Clearly, you do not understand how to run your newspaper. We have a business to run and we can no longer accept your haphazard system of payment. And that is my final word. Good day to you, sir!"

Olivia stepped aside as Mr. Hyde swept by, propelled by his anger. Quentin Tyler looked furious.

"And a good day to you, too, sir!"

Olivia was ready to flee. Then she realized she would immediately have to face Jasper, and he would know her for the coward she was.

"Yes, Miss King?" Quentin Tyler held out his hand. "Is that envelope for me?"

Olivia passed Mr. Tyler the articles and photographs. She turned to go. Mr. Tyler ripped the envelope open.

"Where are you going? I'll read these right now."

Olivia felt a bit faint. She had never imagined that he would read her work—right in front of her!

"Oh, no, that's not necessary, Mr. Tyler."

"Take a seat, Miss King. I may as well do this right now."

Olivia sat down and for the next five minutes endeavored to look everywhere but at Quentin Tyler. The large wall clock was made in Kitchener, Ontario, now wasn't that interesting? That's where Arabella's clock had been made, too. Oh my, thought Olivia, Sara *still* hasn't moved Arabella's clock out of the upstairs hallway. Hetty had mentioned it again last night. And look, there were twenty-four panes of glass in each of the large windows facing the street, and seven notices on the billboard inside the door. Three were for sales of farm machinery, one was for a pie social, two were for boats for sale and one was for a lost cat—"Muffy," by name. Mr. Tyler set the articles down.

"So, these are your exciting stories, are they, Miss King?"

Olivia got up from her chair. "Oh, Mr. Tyler, I wish you could have seen the expression on Pat Frewen's face when that pig of his bolted. It was hilarious!"

"I'm sure it was. Who took the photographs?"

"Jasper Dale," reported Olivia brightly. "Aren't they wonderful?"

Mr. Tyler looked up sharply. "Jasper Dale? I've heard of him. Crack-brained, they say."

"Oh, no, Mr. Tyler," Olivia cried. "He's a very talented photographer, as you can see."

Mr. Tyler put the articles and photographs back in the envelope and handed it to Olivia.

"I can't use these, Miss King." He turned and walked over to the printing press. Olivia followed him.

"But why not?"

Quentin Tyler started to ink the press, his head bent to the task. He didn't look up as he spoke.

"Miss King, the paper is already full of little tidbits like those, and photographs don't make them more exciting. They simply won't sell enough papers to pay for my printing costs, and, as you obviously overheard, that's exactly what I have to do. Good day, Miss King."

Olivia felt helpless and humiliated. It was over. All over. Now she would have to face Jasper, and Sara and, oh Lord, Hetty, and admit that she was a total failure.

Outside, Jasper took one look at Olivia's face and knew that he couldn't press her about what had transpired with Quentin Tyler. He simply helped her up into the buggy, patted her hand and headed Dolly back towards Rose Cottage. Finally Olivia spoke.

"Well, Jasper, he said my articles wouldn't sell

newspapers. He said they just weren't exciting enough." Tears tickled the corners of Olivia's eyes. She looked away.

There was so much Jasper wanted to say, but he ended up with "Oh—that's too b-b-bad." He wanted to kick himself! Olivia looked so forlorn.

"After all that work. And they were such wonderful photographs, too, Jasper. I feel just terrible. You have no idea. I'm so sorry to have troubled you. What a complete waste of your time."

"Oh, no, no, *no*, no—I had a f-f-fine time. Best— in years."

"You don't have to say that, Jasper. Oh, Hetty told me I was an absolute fool, and she was right."

Nothing more was said until they turned up the lane to Rose Cottage. Olivia seemed to brighten a bit.

"Jasper, the least I can do is offer you tea. Do you have time to come in?"

He smiled. "Oh, y-yes, Olivia. I have time."

Sara had seen the buggy pull up and was waiting in the kitchen to meet them.

"Aunt Olivia, Jasper!" she cried, "What did Mr. Tyler say? I can hardly wait to see your articles in print!"

"Well," cautioned Aunt Olivia, going into the hall to hang up her hat, "don't get too excited."

Jasper pulled out a chair and sat down across from Sara at the kitchen table. Here was her chance.

Sara leaned towards him, lowering her voice.

"Jasper, about that blackberry pie that Aunt Olivia brought over for you yesterday?"

"Y-Yes?"

"You haven't said anything to her about it, have you?"

"N-No. Not yet."

"Oh, good! Because I think she wanted it to be a secret. You know, almost as though a good fairy had delivered it. So I really, truly think you shouldn't say anything to her directly about it. I think it would just embarrass her, and that would be dreadful, don't you agree?"

Olivia swung back into the kitchen and started to fill the tea kettle. Sara gave Jasper an inquiring look. He nodded his agreement. Well played, Miss Stanley! thought Sara, as Olivia warmed the large, brown teapot.

"Jasper, do you like your tea weak or strong?"

"Whatever you decide, Olivia, is f-f-fine with me."

Olivia lifted the special Chinese tea caddy down from the second shelf. Jasper leaned back slightly in his chair.

"So, you're feeling better, Sara? R-R-Recovered from your fainting spell?"

"Oh, yes, thank you, Jasper. So much better. You can't imagine! Now please, please, tell me all about Mr. Tyler and what happened."

So Aunt Olivia did just that, as Sara and Jasper listened intently. Sara felt her anger rising, like a high Atlantic tide. How dare Mr. Tyler dismiss Aunt Olivia that way! What a horrible man! What could be done? What could Aunt Olivia write about that would be irrestible to Quentin Tyler and the *Chronicle* readers? But of course! No doubt about it! Sara excused herself, and when she hurried back into the kitchen, she was carrying Arabella's letters and diary. Sara held them aloft.

"Aunt Olivia, here's your story!"

Olivia sighed. "Now what, Sara?"

"I found these yesterday. In the chest. Arabella's diary and a whole bunch of love letters."

"Sara, calm down, one thing at a time. I was there when we cleared out Aunt Arabella's chest, remember? There weren't any letters."

"There was a false bottom, Aunt Olivia! I found it. Actually, I fell through it."

Jasper chuckled. "I'm sorry I missed th- that."

Sara ignored this remark; she fanned through the letters and found the one she wanted.

"This," she confirmed, "this is a letter that Arabella's fiancé wrote to her the night before their wedding. Will couldn't have killed himself, like everyone said, I'm sure of it! He was madly, wonderfully in love with her. All he talked about was their future and how happy they would be together."

Olivia spoke gently. "Sara, no one knows the pain of the inner heart. Who knows what demons Will might have been wrestling with in his deepest soul?"

"Please, Aunt Olivia," Sara begged, "just listen to his own words! The night before the wedding he knew his life was in danger. He told Arabella that—"

Olivia set down her teacup with a clatter.

"Sara, those letters are private. I really don't think you should be reading them."

Sara handed Olivia the red leather diary. "Read it," she urged.

"I think, Olivia," observed Jasper, "that if Arabella truly hadn't wanted anyone to read her letters, she would have d-d-destroyed them."

Olivia had to admit that this made sense. She also had to admit that she was getting more and more curious.

"Very well, Sara. Read away."

Sara cleared her throat.

"'April 28th, 1851. Dearest Arabella: I have distressing news. I have secured my share of the family fortune, but I fear my brother's ill will. He is terribly angry and upset. It is possible that fate may take me from you. Only time will tell. Treasure my wedding gift. Your dearest love always, Will.' See? I told you."

Jasper whistled softly through his teeth.

"Good Lord," whispered Olivia. She opened Arabella's diary and quickly leafed through it to the entry for April 29th, Arabella's wedding day.

"Listen to this. 'I fear that my beloved Will has been murdered by his own brother! I must leave the Island, as my own life may also be in danger. Time will reveal all, and hides the fortune that was rightfully Will's.' "

"I told you!" squealed Sara. "Will was murdered right here in Avonlea."

"Looks like it," admitted Jasper. "And it certainly explains why Arabella left Avonlea so s-s-suddenly."

Sara's eyes shone. "It's an incredible story, but there's still a treasure to be found, I'm sure of that now. Where can it be hidden?"

Jasper's chin was set at a determined angle.

"Sara's right. This *is* a r-r-ripping story. Even Quentin Tyler couldn't turn this one down."

"But I don't even know who Will was, or anything about him, or..." Olivia remembered the closed look on Quentin Tyler's face.

"Well," suggested Jasper, "The n-n-newspaper archives would be a good place to start. Check the vitals—the births and deaths."

"You can do it, Aunt Olivia," insisted Sara. "Never give up, that's what you always tell me."

Aunt Olivia erased Quentin Tyler's cold expression from her mind. After all, what was life without a challenge? Isn't that what she had said she wanted?

"All right. I'll do it."

Sara gave Aunt Olivia a big hug as Jasper went outside to unhitch Dolly.

As Sara and Jasper waited outside the *Chronicle*'s offices, Olivia once again confronted Quentin Tyler, who was at the press, counting freshly printed auction notices.

"Sixty-one, sixty-two—" He glanced up at Olivia. "Forget something, Miss King?"

Olivia cleared her throat.

Quentin Tyler droned on, ignoring her. "Sixty-three, sixty-four—"

"Mr. Tyler, I'd like you to give me a second chance. I think my niece and I have uncovered an amazing story. One of great human drama."

Tyler paused, his inky fingers marking his place.

"Now don't tell me. The town cat had kittens."

"Please, Mr. Tyler," said Olivia. "I'm extremely serious."

"Well, I have to give you credit, Miss King. You don't give up easily....All right. You've got your second chance."

"Good! Now, I'll need access to your files—your archives," Olivia requested.

Mr. Tyler gestured with his thumb toward two

wooden file cabinets at the back of the office. He returned to his counting. "Sixty-five, sixty-six—"

"Mr. Tyler, where will I find the obituaries, pardon me, the vitals, for 1851? April, 1851?"

"Try that cabinet in the corner. Sixty-seven, sixty-eight —"

She had her second chance! She'd fought for it and won it. Olivia found herself almost writing the story aloud as she looked in the files for April, 1851.

"Although many consider Avonlea to be a rather unexciting place," she said to no one in particular, "for fifty years she has hidden a dramatic tale—a tale of lost treasure, of deep hatred between brothers—of a love story that ended in murder, violent and unbidden."

Olivia didn't see Quentin Tyler's face darken as he looked up from his counting and realized what she was saying. He strode over to the filing cabinet, reached across the file drawer and closed it decisively, almost catching Olivia's fingers.

"I've changed my mind, Miss King. Please leave immediately."

"But Mr. Tyler, you said I—"

Quentin Tyler's jaw was set. "What I'm saying now is that you must leave immediately, Miss King. Do I make myself clear?"

Olivia had no intention of being further insulted. "Crystal clear, Mr. Tyler," she replied, as she marched towards the door and closed it, just a whisker shy of a slam, on her way out.

"Well, Olivia," said Jasper, as Dolly trotted down the road, "it certainly sounds to me as if he doesn't want you to know what's in the f-f-files."

"It's unfair," growled Sara. "It's just the type of story he said he wanted. And you certainly can't write it without more information."

Disappointment thickened Olivia's words. "It was stupid of me to think that I could do it. Hetty was right this time. I can just hear what *she's* going to say."

Jasper spoke quietly. "You can't l-listen to what everyone says. You have to—you have to do what's right for you. And I think—I do think you can do just about anything you set your mind to, Olivia."

Olivia looked unconvinced. Jasper pulled up the buggy in front of Rose Cottage. Jasper hopped down first, and then Sara. Jasper offered Olivia his hand.

"D-Don't you go giving up now, Olivia."

"Jasper, don't you see it's all over?"

"Oh, I d-d-don't think it has to be."

Olivia spoke unusually crisply. "Yes, it does have to be! It's over, Jasper. I tried and I failed. End of story. Now, please, just leave me alone. I mean it." She walked quickly into the house, not looking back.

Poor Jasper looked quite devastated. "I—I

forgot to pick up the m-m-mail downtown," he muttered to Sara as he wearily got back up on the buggy.

Sara watched as Jasper turned Dolly down the lane. The buggy disappeared into the shimmering afternoon. The course of true love never did run smooth, thought Sara, quoting the words of the great Shakespeare. Well, almost never. Then Sara had a brilliant thought. She smiled as she went into the house. It was nice, having brilliant thoughts. Jasper and Aunt Olivia would be together, if she had anything to do with it. They would be Mr. and Mrs. Dale, and no doubt about it!

Chapter Twelve

"So—Jasper Dale's seeing you home now, is he?" As Sara paused in the hallway, she could hear Hetty setting the table for supper. Olivia's reply rose above the tinkle of plates and cutlery. There was an edge to her voice.

"Is there anything wrong with that, Hetty?"

"Really, Olivia, there's no need to get huffy. I'm merely suggesting that perhaps it would be best if you were...a little more discriminating." A plate banged down. Oh, thought Sara, it was Aunt Olivia setting the table.

"Perhaps it would be best if you mind your business and I mind mine, Hetty."

"Oh, of course," replied Hetty, "your business. And just how is your so-called business going?"

"If it's all the same to you," said Olivia resolutely, "I think I'd rather not discuss it. I don't think I could endure your gloating!" Olivia moved towards the door.

Hetty called after her. "Gloating? I'm not gloating. Really, Olivia, what's got into you?"

Olivia brushed past Sara and vanished up the stairs. Sara edged towards the front door, hoping Aunt Hetty wouldn't spot her. No such luck.

"Sara? Is that you? Where have you been?"

"Oh, hello, Aunt Hetty," chirped Sara, as Hetty poked her head around the door. "I was just on my way out."

"Your way out? Sara, you're supposed to be in bed."

"Aunt Hetty, I am fully recovered. Truly. All morning I rested and drank beef tea, just as you said I should."

"Well, you do look much perkier, child."

Sara moved towards the door. "So I think a little walk would do me good."

"Well, dinner's in half an hour, so don't be long. I mean it now."

Sara grinned. "I'll be back in time. You have my word."

Aunt Hetty sighed as Sara raced down the path. Olivia upstairs, tearful and upset, Sara fainting and recovering. Ever since Aunt Arabella's blue chest had been opened, strange things had been happening, for reasons Hetty couldn't quite put her finger on.

Sara hammered on the kitchen door of the King farm. Felix opened the door, but before he could say hello, Sara was in the kitchen.

"Hey," Felix hollered, "what's going on?"

"Felicity," announced Sara dramatically, "I need food. Desperately. Right now." Felicity looked up from the table, where she was struggling over her seven times-multiplications.

Felix started to laugh. "I thought you were still full from Ma's big dinner. You sure ate enough, Sara Stanley."

"Felicity, I mean it. What have you got that I can take away and eat?"

Felicity looked puzzled. "Eat?"

Really, Felicity could be dim. "Eat! Eat!" Sara was almost shouting.

"Felicity made a nice lemon loaf this morning," Cecily offered quietly.

"Good," said Sara. "Where is it?"

Cecily enjoyed being helpful. "In the pantry. I'll get it for you, Sara."

Felicity grabbed Cecily's pinafore as she went by. "Just a minute, Cecily. Sara, what will you give me for my lemon loaf? I mean, you can't just march in here and demand things without payment."

"That's right," added Felix. "Fair's fair."

Sara decided they had a point. "I'll give you my blue satin hair ribbon."

"Not enough," said Felicity. "I want your pink hankie, too. The one with the little daisies embroidered on it."

Sara groaned. Her father had sent her that hankie on her last birthday. Oh well, love was worth anything. Sara gritted her teeth and nodded.

"And a week's supply of Cupids," demanded Felicity.

Sara reached into her pocket and flung a handful of the candies on the table. Felicity let go of Cecily's pinafore.

"Get her the lemon loaf, Cecily. And Sara, you have to tell us what's going on. You're acting most peculiar."

"Later," called Sara, hurrying out the door with the lemon loaf. "All will be revealed later!"

Next stop, Golden Milestone. Sara raced up the path, brushing past the lilacs and flowering hawthorn. This time she didn't have to worry about whether or not Jasper Dale was home. He was definitely in town, at the post office. Sara's mission was clear and precise. She must leave the lemon loaf, as a peace offering, where Jasper would find it. He would know it was from Olivia, and all would be well.

Sara set the loaf down on the little table beside the front door. Wait a minute? How would he know it was from Olivia? It wasn't like the pie, which had been clearly marked with a "K." Think, think, think. Very well, Sara would have to leave a note. Well, not a note, just a slip of paper that said, "Sorry— Olivia." Surely Sara could forge Olivia's signature. Of course she could.

Sara opened the front door of Jasper Dale's house and slipped inside. Paper and pens would be in the study. Sara was at the foot of the stairs, about to enter the study, when she paused. Up those stairs and to the left was the secret room. Suddenly, Sara's curiosity bubbled up, wild and uncontrollable. After all, she would just look, that's all. It wasn't as though she was going to take anything. And perhaps the secret room might be where she would find just the right paper and pen to write Aunt Olivia's note to Jasper. At least, that's what Sara told herself as she mounted the stairs.

It was strange, but Sara felt impelled to knock softly before she opened the door. Did she really expect to find someone there? Of course, there was no answer, and Sara opened the door.

She found herself in a finely furnished room. Delicate lace curtains hung before the square, broad-silled windows. The walls were adorned with fine pictures, and between the windows was a bookcase filled with beautifully bound books. Beside it stood a little table with a dainty work-basket on it. By the basket Sara saw a pair of tiny scissors and a silver thimble. A wicker rocking chair, comfortable with cushions, was near it. A vase of mayflowers stood on top of the bookcase. This was a lady's room, in every subtle way, and Sara's young heart knew it. All this was astonishing enough, but what puzzled Sara completely was the fact that a woman's dress—a pale, silken frock—was hanging over a chair before the mirror. And on the floor beside it were two blue satin slippers! Whose room was this?

"Miss Stanley? I don't recall inviting you in."

Sara spun around, her hand at her throat. Jasper Dale was looking at her, with a steady, serious gaze. Sara gasped. Obviously, she had been so taken with the room that she hadn't heard him come up the stairs! Sara opened her mouth to speak, but no words formed. Jasper spoke softly, almost regretfully, and without a trace of a stutter.

"I am bitterly disappointed in you, Sara. I thought you had the soul of a poet. I thought you understood the need for privacy and for private thoughts. Obviously, I was wrong. I think it's best if you go now. I really have nothing else to say to you."

Hot tears blinded Sara as she stumbled down the stairs. What had she done! She was a fool—the lowest of the low. As she trudged home in the deepening twilight, Jasper's words rang in her aching heart and head. If only he had shouted in anger, the way Uncle Alec might have. Somehow, that would have been easier to bear than the quiet anguish reflected on Jasper's plain face. "Bitterly disappointed..." Oh, that was horrible. It was one thing to make someone angry, but quite another to bitterly disappoint them. Sara had intruded, terribly, into Jasper's secret world. He was right, she didn't have the soul of a poet and oh, oh, that hurt to hear.

That evening, Sara picked morosely at her dinner and went up to her room early. Olivia and Hetty thought she was still tired from her stomach trouble and her fainting spell, so they tucked her in, grateful that she was getting some much-needed rest.

Sara lay on her bed, miserable, staring at the ceiling. She felt dazed and exhausted, too dispirited even to take her daily dose of Cupids. Somehow, sometime, she would have to apologize to Jasper. But right now she just wanted to blot the secret room, and everything that had happened there, out of her mind.

Later in the evening, Olivia slipped out the door and walked, in the soft darkness, to Golden Milestone. Sara didn't hear her leave because, by that time, she had fallen into a restless, wretched, dream-drenched sleep.

The next day Sara woke up feeling somewhat better. Towards morning she had slept more or less peacefully. After all, what had happened at Golden Milestone was just a matter of her curiosity overtaking her, she told herself. It was wrong, certainly, but it wasn't, as Aunt Hetty would say, "villainous."

By the time Sara came home from school, her thoughts were once again turning to Arabella's letters and the lost treasure. The same curiosity that had propelled her into the secret room found Sara sitting on her bed in the early evening with Olivia, puzzling over the old letters and the diary.

Olivia frowned. "Sara, we *must* be missing something. Read me that part at the end of the diary again."

Sara flipped to the last page. "'Time will reveal all, and hides the fortune that was rightfully Will's.'" Sara looked puzzled. "I still don't understand."

Olivia shuffled the letters and found the one she wanted. "The thing is, Sara, that Will said almost the same thing in his last letter to Arabella. Listen— 'Fate may take me from you. Only time will tell. Treasure my wedding gift.'" Olivia set the letter down. "What does it mean? *Time* will tell. *Time* will reveal all.'"

"They have to be clues," moaned Sara. "But what do they point to? What do they mean?"

As Sara and Olivia looked at each other, mystified, Hetty's voice pierced their mood.

"Ouch! Drat and double-drat!!" Sara's door flew open and Hetty marched in, scowling. She was carrying Aunt Arabella's clock, which she placed, with a thump, on Sara's dresser.

"It's beyond me what's going on in this house anymore, but if it's of any interest to either of you, dinner is ready. And Sara, if you want to save this clock from the scrap heap, kindly leave it in your room. I am tired of stubbing my toe on it in the hall- way!" Aunt Hetty wheeled around, her straight back heading for the door.

"Aunt Hetty!" Sara screeched, "Wait! That's it, Aunt Olivia! *'Time* will tell! Treasure my wedding gift!' *'Time* will reveal all, and hides the fortune that was Will's!' "

Hetty looked confused. "What on earth are you babbling about?"

Olivia jumped up and hugged Hetty, as Sara danced around. "Oh, Hetty," whooped Olivia, "you're wonderful! Of course, the clock—time!—the treasure must be hidden in the clock!!"

Olivia scooped up the clock and raced down the stairs, with Sara on her heels. Hetty stood at the landing, shouting that she didn't understand.

"We'll explain everything later," Olivia yelled up, "but right now we have to leave. Come along, Sara."

"Where are we going?"

Olivia was halfway out the door. "To Jasper Dale's, of course!"

Sara's heart dropped a mile. "To Jasper Dale's?" she croaked.

Hetty clattered down the stairs and joined them at the front door. "Why on earth are you going to Jasper Dale's, Olivia?" she demanded.

Olivia spoke as though Sara and Hetty were rather dense. "So that he can take the clock apart and find the treasure, that's why. Now let's get going!"

Hetty grabbed her hat. "You're not going without me. Sara, come along. We'll all go together."

Hetty and Olivia marched briskly down the lane, as Sara trotted to keep up, wondering how she could face Jasper after their dreadful encounter in the secret room.

And so it was that Rose Cottage was empty when Quentin Tyler arrived an hour later, determined to find out exactly what Olivia King knew about his uncle, Will Tyler, and the tragic events of fifty years ago.

When Sara begged Aunt Hetty to let her run on ahead to Golden Milestone, Aunt Hetty indulged her, thinking that it was Sara's "natural high spirits."

Jasper Dale was working in his garden, catching the last of the daylight, as Sara panted to a halt by the fence. Sara prayed that when she spoke, she would say the right thing—or something close to the right thing. Her heart was tripping and it wasn't just from running. Jasper lowered his pruning shears and observed Sara. He waited for her to speak. She started in, her voice shaky.

"Mr. Dale, I am so very, very sorry for what happened yesterday, sorrier than you'll ever know. I had no right to intrude that way, no right at all." She paused. Would he ever, ever forgive her? He looked so serious, so unrelenting. "Please, Mr. Dale, please accept my apology."

Jasper walked over to the fence. He held out his hand. "I accept your apology, Sara." They shook hands gravely. Sara almost collapsed with relief. As difficult as this was, at least it was done. She wouldn't have any more of those horrible dreams and horrible feelings. It would take her a while to get over it, but she felt now that at least there was hope.

Jasper was surprisingly poised as Olivia and Hetty descended on him, imploring his assistance in opening the old clock. He brewed them a strong pot of tea and offered them lemon loaf, which Sara couldn't eat. Soon they were all gathered around the kitchen table, watching Jasper pry the clock open. Even Aunt Hetty looked quite sparkly, Sara thought. Everyone loves a mystery!

"But I still don't understand," Hetty complained.

"It's true," Olivia confirmed, "Arabella's fiancé, Will, was murdered."

"His treasure is hidden in the clock," Sara added brightly. She really was feeling so much better.

Hetty sniffed. "I've never heard such hogwash in my life."

"Hogwash isn't a very genteel w-w-word, Miss King," Jasper noted, working to remove the back of the clock. Hetty looked rather surprised, as though a bumblebee had landed on her arm. Olivia laughed. Sara smiled.

"Is there anything in the clock, Mr. Dale?" Sara asked.

"I don't rightly know. Can't quite s-s-see yet."

"For heaven's sake, Jasper," snapped Hetty, "either there's something in there or there isn't!"

Jasper carefully removed the back of the clock and reached in. "Wait—wait—no, I don't th-think— yes, there is something in here."

Sara's eyes widened. "I knew it! I just knew it!"

Jasper removed a small object and placed it on the table.

"Oh, no," howled Sara, "it's only the winding key."

"What did I tell you," Hetty said frostily, "treasure indeed."

But Jasper was still groping in the clock, reaching further into its deep base. "Now, just a—oh my, here now—"

"What, Jasper! What!" Hetty was almost shouting. Jasper looked up and grinned as he removed a black leather pouch. Everyone leaned in, breathing as one. Jasper opened the pouch. Diamond brooches, ruby rings, an emerald necklace, a gold watch, fine gold chains and unset gems spilled out on the table! It was incredible! Sara could hardly believe what she was seeing!

"Jewels," she breathed, "real jewels."

Aunt Hetty reached into the pouch and pulled out a roll of old documents. She started to read them. Her eyes widened.

"These are mining shares. Good heavens, each one is worth five hundred dollars and there are— there must be at least ten deeds here!"

Aunt Olivia picked up one of the deeds and read aloud from the back of it.

"'William Tyler—one hundred shares. Five hundred dollars total value.' This was Will's gift to Arabella, his name on it proves it beyond a shadow of a doubt!"

"Miss King," said a voice from the door. "You turned into quite a clever reporter, didn't you." Everyone gasped as Quentin Tyler moved into the room. "But I'm afraid your exciting story will never be seen in print."

Jasper stood up. "Explain yourself, sir," he demanded boldly, "or you can show yourself out by the way you came in!"

Quentin Tyler removed his hat. He didn't look as though he were leaving.

"Forgive me, but the door was open."

"Oh, my!" exclaimed Hetty, to no one in particular.

"An open door is no excuse," said Jasper, sternly. "Now go on, get out of here!"

Olivia stepped forward, putting a restraining hand on Jasper's arm. "Jasper, this is Mr. Tyler from the Avonlea *Chronicle*."

Mr. Tyler regarded Olivia darkly. "Miss King, I will not allow you to drag my father's name through the mud. What's past is past."

Olivia's eyes widened. "Your father was Will's brother?"

Mr. Tyler nodded. "And he, too, was in love with your Aunt Arabella."

"So your father murdered Will," declared Sara.

"He didn't murder Will," Mr. Tyler countered.

Sara held her ground. "Oh yes he did. He wanted Will's share of the family fortune. It says so in his letter and in Arabella's diary."

Mr. Tyler shook his head. "No, no. They got into a fight. They struggled. Will's gun went off accidentally. It wasn't murder, it was an accident."

Aunt Hetty decided to deal with this impertinent intruder.

"So you've come to claim the treasure, I suppose."

"Ah, yes," said Mr. Tyler ruefully, walking towards the mound of jewellery winking on the table, "the family treasure. My father lived with guilt his whole life. If there's one thing I remember from his misery, it's that having money isn't worth the price it exacts from your soul. I want nothing to do with blood money."

Aunt Hetty was unimpressed. "Don't try to sell me that bill of goods, Mr. Tyler." She addressed the room in her best lecturing style. "He didn't come here merely to protect his father's name— no, not at all! Mr. Tyler, I know your kind. You've allowed these people to do your dirty work for you, and now you want to reap the rewards."

Quentin Tyler opened his mouth, attempting to speak. Hetty soared on.

"Well, why else would you break in here and terrify us as you have? I have a good mind to send for Constable Jeffries!"

"Hetty, really," Olivia chided, "no one is that terrified. Mr. Tyler, as Will's heir, the treasure is rightfully yours. Please take it."

"Have you taken leave of your senses, Olivia!" Hetty barked. "These jewels have been under the King roof for the past fifty years. Whatever are you thinking of!"

Jasper spoke very calmly. "Hetty, I believe Olivia to be in the right. The treasure belongs in the Tyler family, however much you may not l-l-like it."

"Hush up, Jasper," said Hetty smartly, "this is a family matter."

Sara was really starting to enjoy this.

"Hetty, this is not just a family matter," snapped Olivia. "Jasper is more a part of this than you are. How dare you interfere!"

"Oh, I'll interfere if I see fit, my girl."

"I can handle this perfectly well by myself," Olivia said evenly.

"Oh, how could you, Olivia," Aunt Hetty sniffed. "You've no judgment."

"I have had just about enough of you telling me what I have and what I don't have," replied Olivia defiantly. "So I would appreciate it if you would stop and think for a change, before uttering another bit of your advice for my own good!"

Hetty turned away, speechless, the color drained from her face.

Olivia gestured to the treasure. "Mr. Tyler, this is yours. Please take it."

"But I told you—"

Olivia spoke in reasoned tones. "Mr. Tyler, your father's newspaper is in trouble. Invest in it. Give those Charlottetown papers a run for their money. And you did say that if I found an exciting story, I could write it. It will do no harm for the truth to be told now."

Jasper addressed Mr. Tyler, quietly. "And isn't that what newspapers are all about, Mr. T-T—"

"Tyler," prompted Aunt Hetty, having found her voice again.

"Yes, quite," said Jasper. "Aren't newspapers all about the truth?"

There was a silence. The cold look in Quentin Tyler's eyes started to melt. It must be a great relief for him to finally have this family secret out in the open, thought Sara.

"You may write your story, Olivia," Mr. Tyler said quietly, "and I would be honored to print it."

"Well," said Aunt Hetty, after Quentin Tyler had left, "I must say, after all is said and done, this has been quite an exciting evening. But we really should be on our way. I have arithmetic tests to mark before tomorrow."

"Oh, can't we stay just a little while?" pleaded Sara, "there's still so much to talk about."

Aunt Olivia sipped her tea. "Hetty, you go on ahead. Sara and I will be along shortly." Although the two sisters hadn't apologized to each other, they both recognized that in the heat of the moment, they had said things they otherwise might have kept to themselves.

"If you don't mind then," said Hetty, "I think I will get along." She peered at Jasper and acknowledged, rather stiffly, "Thank you, for your help. And for the tea. And the lemon loaf."

"You're most w-w-welcome," Jasper replied graciously, seeing Hetty to the door.

Once Hetty was safely on her way, Jasper poured the last of the tea and passed round the plate of lemon loaf. After another fifteen minutes of amiable conversation Olivia and Sara, too, said their goodbyes.

It was a lovely, velvet-warm night. Frogs chorused from their mossy platforms in ponds beside the road. A cow lowed in a nearby meadow while, in the distance, an owl hooted softly to the dark blue sky. There was an easy silence between Sara and Aunt Olivia as they strolled towards Rose Cottage, but as they walked, anxiety started to nip at Sara's heels. She knew she had to speak.

"Aunt Olivia, there's something I must tell you."

Aunt Olivia spoke gently. "I know."

Sara stared into the dark. "What—do you know?"

"I know how much you want to see Jasper and I together, in love—even married."

"Oh," said Sara, faintly.

"And I understand that, my dear. And even though you love your own father deeply, I know how much you would like a real family. But the thing is, Sara, that's your dream."

Sara found her voice. "But you always said I should have dreams, Aunt Olivia."

"And so you should, Sara. But you can't force other people to make your dreams come true."

Sara gulped. "The pie...?" Sara could hear the smile in her Aunt Olivia's voice.

"Jasper saw you from the upstairs window."

"And the secret room?"

"Jasper told me about the room, but I haven't seen it. Maybe I never will. All I know is that it's waiting for someone special, but even Jasper isn't sure who that will be. So his secret must stay safe with you, Sara."

"Oh, it will!" howled Sara, "I promise!" She flung herself into Olivia's forgiving arms.

Olivia stroked Sara's hair, holding her close and warm. "There, there, my dear, there, there."

Sara sobbed, her young heart overflowing. After a bit, Olivia produced a fresh handerkerchief and dabbed Sara's tears away. Sara blew her nose. She was starting to feel better. They continued to walk, hand in hand.

"I really like Jasper very much," confided Olivia, "but love has to grow in its own way, and in its own time. You understand, don't you?"

"Oh, yes. I do," said Sara. And she truly, finally did.

Chapter Thirteen

A noisy celebration was underway in the kitchen of Rose Cottage. As Aunt Olivia exuberantly filled glasses with her splendid punch, Hetty sat off to one side, reading the current issue of the Avonlea *Chronicle*.

Sara knew the front-page article practically by heart! It was all about the Tyler treasure and the amazing events that led up to its discovery. But the thing was, in addition to Olivia's article, there was the most terrific photograph right there on the front page. Jasper had taken a dandy picture of Sara and Olivia standing in the dining room of Rose Cottage, with the clock and the treasure on the table in front of them. They were smiling from ear to ear.

Felix stuffed another sugar cookie in his mouth. "Who would have thought there would be treasure in that old clock?"

"Felix, don't talk with your mouth full," scolded Felicity.

"It ain't full!"

"You really shouldn't say 'ain't,' " Cecily added, quite nicely, "should he?"

"Now, children," warned Aunt Janet. "don't fight."

"I'm only sorry I couldn't f-f-fix that old clock," said Jasper.

"I'm only sorry I didn't keep it," confessed Alec.

Everyone laughed. Everyone except Aunt Hetty, that is, who had her nose buried in the newspaper.

"Come, come, Hetty," teased Alec King. "Where's your sense of humor? You're far too much like Grandmother King, you know. Now, Grandfather King, he was the one with the get-up-and-go. You're starting to remind me of him, Olivia."

Olivia smiled. She looked so lovely tonight, thought Sara, dressed in her pretty muslin dress, the very same one she had worn to Jasper's the day she asked him to take the photographs for her, the day....Now stop it, Sara reminded herself. Let Jasper and Olivia's story tell itself.

Hetty excused herself and left the kitchen to answer a knock at the front door.

Janet King sighed. "Poor Arabella. Imagine hiding a secret like that all her life."

"Well, if Sara hadn't stumbled on all those old letters, we would never have known," Olivia assured them.

"It's true," said Felicity, only slightly reluctant. "I think I probably do owe Sara a hen's tooth."

Sara grinned. Felicity wasn't all that bad. And since nothing more had been said about Sara's blue hair ribbon and the pink hankie, it seemed Felicity wasn't going to collect on her barter for the lemon loaf.

"Ahem," coughed Hetty, as she ushered Quentin Tyler into the kitchen.

Olivia held out her hand in a warm greeting. "Oh, Mr. Tyler, what a delightful surprise. Will you join us in a glass of punch?"

"No, no, I really can't stay. I—well, I just want to thank you."

Olivia blushed. "Thank me?"

Mr. Tyler presented Olivia with a long, narrow, leather-bound box. He bowed slightly. "I want you to have this." He produced a similar box and, to Sara's astonishment and delight, handed it to her!

"Oh, Mr. Tyler, you needn't have done this," said Olivia.

"I know," said Mr. Tyler, "but I wanted to. Greed has led the Tyler family into trouble once too often."

Sara opened the lid on the box. She lifted out a delicately wrought gold chain. Hanging from it was a beautifully set moonstone, pale and mysterious.

"Oh, Sara, look at it!" squealed Cecily.

"Oh, thank you, Mr. Tyler," said Sara earnestly. "It's—well, it's almost poetic."

Mr. Tyler smiled. Felix groaned. Poetic! Jumping Jehoshaphat!! Aunt Olivia held up an exquisite hairpin, patterned with tiny rubies and diamonds.

"Mr. Tyler, this is *extremely* generous of you."

"Oh, not really. I've sold more newspapers in the last few days than I have in months. I guess it just goes to show that people will still buy a small town newspaper if there's some excitement in it."

"I'm very pleased for you," said Olivia warmly.

"But I realize," continued Mr. Tyler, "that a paper is only as good as its writers. I'm thinking of hiring someone on a more permanent basis and I was wondering if you would be interested, Miss King?"

Olivia broke into a smile. "Yes, I'd be most interested, Mr. Tyler."

"Good, good. The Avonlea *Chronicle* welcomes you with open arms."

Olivia raised a warning finger. "However, I'll only accept the job if I can bring along my talented photographer."

Mr. Tyler agreed. "Of course." Jasper looked immensely pleased and gave Olivia one of those special smiles.

Alec raised his glass high. "Well now, I think this calls for a toast."

"No, no," blared Janet, "Alec, wait."

"I'm waiting," said Alec.

Janet collected her thoughts. "Yes, well now. Hetty is the eldest. As head of the family, I think she should propose Olivia's toast. Hetty?"

Aunt Hetty looked surprised as she slowly rose to her feet. She cleared her throat.

"Well, I must say, I'm—well, I'm still slightly dazed by the unexpected events of the last few days, but be that as it may, Olivia, I am not one to withhold credit where credit is due and, I must say, you do have a talent for stories." Hetty reached for her punch glass and raised it high. "I found your newspaper story a far more compelling read than—"

"'Season's End?'" offered Jasper, from the corner.

"Yes, quite. The truth is, Olivia, I couldn't put it down, and the photograph is—good. So, here is to your continued success in whatever it is you set your mind to do. To Olivia!"

Everyone raised their glasses in a heartfelt toast to Olivia, and the evening continued on its merry course until the wee hours of the morning.

Sara put on her nightgown, yawned and contemplated the bowl of Cupids on her bedside table. Cupids were fine, she thought, but she really didn't need them anymore. Not before she went to sleep, anyway.

Sara drifted to her window and gazed out at the full moon floating, like a crystal, above the rim of the dark pine forest. Everyone in Avonlea would be asleep now—Aunt Janet and Uncle Alec snoring a duet in their dark oak bed; Felicity and Cecily in their gabled room; Aunt Hetty and Aunt Olivia in their shadowed spaces; Jasper Dale slumbering in the bachelor tidiness of Golden Milestone. And Sara finally knew that all of these folk were, in some deep, unspoken way, her family.

Sara slipped into bed, whispered goodnight to the dear dark and closed her eyes. She slept sweetly, dreaming her own dreams, at peace with the world, and in her heart.